Rusty Wilson's

....

Eighteen Pack
of Bigfoot Campfire Stories

I've spent many a night scared to death after hearing some of these tales, but in all honesty, what would life be without mysteries like Bigfoot? —Rusty Wilson

• F O R •

Diana

Contents

Foreword

· ·

by Rusty Wilson

Greetings, fellow adventurers, to this set of eighteen Bigfoot campfire stories, stories guaranteed to either make you smile or scare the socks off you. I've put this collection together for those of you who enjoy the craziness and scariness of Bigfootery and are ready for more hijinks.

This book is a compilation of two of my ebooks: *Rusty Wilson's Six Pack of Bigfoot Campfire Stories* and *Rusty Wilson's Twelve Pack of Bigfoot Campfire Stories*. I've combined them into a book for those of you who don't have ebook readers or for those who just want to have them in print. They've quickly become some of my favorites.

These stories were collected around many campfires, where my flyfishing clients regaled and scared me to death with their Bigfoot encounters. I've spent many a night scared to death after hearing some of these tales, but in all honesty, what would life be like without mysteries like Bigfoot?

So, pull up a chair or log, kick back with some hot chocolate, and be prepared to read some tales that will make your hair stand on end—or maybe make you wonder if you might like to meet the Big Guy himself.

[1] The Bigfoot Avalanche

• •

Flyfishing is a mellow sport, and I sometimes get the older crowd looking for something they can engage with outdoors but not kill themselves doing. This fellow, Ross, really enjoyed flyfishing and was a quick study, even though he had to be in his late 70s. And he told a darn good story, too. This was told over a campfire not far from where it happened, along the Yampa River in northwest Colorado. —Rusty

I've never told this story to anyone before tonight except my daughter. I've always figured people would say I was nuts. Maybe I am, but nuts or not, I know what I saw.

This was when I was young, in my twenties, some fifty years back. I may be an old guy now, but the vision of what I saw is clear as a bell in my mind's eye, and I'll never forget it. I can still relive every second of that event as if it had just happened, even though I can't remember what I had for breakfast. So, I'll get on with the story. I'm curious to know what you think.

This happened one very cold winter day on Juniper Mountain in northwest Colorado. Juniper Mountain isn't even quite 8,000 feet above sea level, which makes it more of a hill by Colorado standards, but it's called Juniper Mountain and is really a big rugged piece of landscape. It looks like something out of a Zane Grey book, with its big rugged slopes covered by junipers and sagebrush, with gullies making their way down from the top.

I was working in a small gravel pit there not too far off Highway 40, and it was the middle of a typical bitter cold Moffat County winter. It was right before Christmas, and I remember this because we were working until the weather shut us down, and that just happened to be a couple of weeks right after this happened, which was at Christmas.

I was running the loader, filling up the county trucks with gravel. The county had hired a bunch of us to do this seasonal job, and all of us were looking forward to getting it done so we could quit for the winter. There were about ten trucks that would come and go all day long, so I kept busy. The county was graveling some of the back roads that the ranchers needed, and everything was way behind, so we were putting in long hours, trying to get done before the weather changed.

My daughter's pretty good on the computer, and last time I was over to her place, she pulled up this program that lets you go see places like from an airplane. I think it was called Google Earth. Anyway, we cruised over there to Juniper Mountain, and if you take a look, you can still see the old gravel pit I was working there off the county road a bit from Highway 40, on the northeast edge of the mountain.

Most of the guys were staying in an old motel in the little town of Maybell, just down the road a bit, but I opted to camp out, as I wanted to save my money. Everyone said I was crazy because it was so cold, but what's new? I grew up in that damn cold country, had spent my life on a ranch, and I was pretty hardy. Plus I was young and stupid.

My mom let me take an old featherbed out there with me, which was great for insulation under me, and I had a big army surplus canvas tent with a small wood stove, so I wasn't doing too bad, even though it was getting down below zero every night. Once I got to bed and got things warmed up, I slept pretty OK. It was getting into bed in the evenings and getting back up in the mornings that was the hard part, because it would be hard to get warmed up in either direction.

Well, we had Sundays off, and my folks' ranch was clear down by Hayden, which was a good 40 or so miles away, and I hated to drive home just for one day. My old pickup was on its last legs, and I didn't have any reason to go there anyway, as they would just put me to work on what was supposed to be my day off.

So I would just hang around on Sundays, reading old dime Westerns and trying to stay warm. We'd had quite a bit of snow back in late November, and it had melted off the roads so we could still work, but the nearby hills were pretty snowed in with a foot or so, and it was even deeper up on Juniper Mountain.

Well, one Sunday I decided I was damn bored and I needed to go do something, especially something that would help me stay warm. It was a beautiful crisp winter day, blue skies and frost hanging in the air. I'd seen the flanks of Juniper Mountain up behind me since I'd started the job, and that day I just decided I wanted to go walk up it and see the view from the top.

I found out later there's an old dirt road that climbs up it from the other side, but that was too far from where I was at anyway. I just headed straight out and started climbing. There was snow on the ground, but it had crusted enough that I could walk on top of it mostly, and it wasn't more than a foot deep anyway, so I just plowed on through the sagebrush and up the side of that mountain. The top was maybe two or three thousand feet above me at the most.

Well, looks can be deceiving when you scope something out from a distance, and sure enough, the mountain had some pretty good gullies going here and there that I had to navigate my way through, mostly just climbing down one side and back up the other. Of course, the snow was deeper in the shadowy side of things, as the sun doesn't get far enough north to melt things that time of year, so some of the gullies were kind of hard to get back out of.

I had stuck a couple of sandwiches in my pocket, and when I finally made it about two-thirds up the mountain, I sat down on a rock and had lunch. Of course, as I climbed higher in altitude, the snow got deeper, and by this time I was about to give it up, as the snow was now a couple of feet deep and hard going, and it was now getting into late afternoon.

I just sat there, eating and enjoying the views, which were pretty good. That country out there is still pretty wild, and there really aren't many people around. It's sheep and cattle country, and in winter about all you ever see is the occasional rancher driving into town for groceries. And back then, it was even less populated. It's a big sky kind of place, lots of barren sagebrush hills and pronghorn antelope. Feels like you're in Wyoming instead of Colorado.

I just sat there, figuring I would head back down, when things changed all of a sudden. I started feeling like I was being watched. It was the darndest thing, sitting up there on the side of that mountain, nobody around for miles, in the snow, feeling like something's watching you. It didn't make much sense, but then I started wondering if a mountain lion might be around.

That country has mountain lions at its higher elevations, where there are deer and such, so I figured that must be what was spooking me. It's not bear country, as it's too dry and bears need water, but a big cat can range pretty far, and the Yampa River wasn't all that far away. But all the deer were now in the lower country, so why would a lion hang around up there?

I stood up slowly and started looking all around, trying to spot where a lion might be hiding. I figured it must be up above me, as there were a couple of small rock cliffs towards the top of the mountain. I turned and scouted those cliffs, but couldn't see anything, but I know lions blend in with their background pretty darn well.

For the life of me, that feeling of being watched just kept getting stronger, but I couldn't see any reason for it. I was getting so uncomfortable that I decided I'd better head on out. I had an old rifle down in my tent, but it sure wasn't going to do me any good up there.

I stood up to go when I heard it. It sounded like a woman screaming, like she was being murdered, and I know cougars make a sound like that, I'd heard it myself more than once back on the ranch. So, at first I thought, yep, a mountain lion, so get out now but don't run, as that triggers their kill instinct.

I started down the side of that mountain, and the snow was deep enough that I was almost skiing down it. Then I heard the sound again, like a woman screaming, but this time it was different. It ended in a deep bass sound and it wasn't like any cougar I'd ever heard. I swear, the sound just hung there in the frost crystals like a cloud, it just went on and on with incredible volume and lung capacity, even though it came from the distance.

Uh oh, I was completely out of my element here. My mind kept saying it's a cougar, but the rest of me said that ain't no cougar, that's something you've never encountered before and you don't want to. I grew up out in that wild country, and this was a sound completely new to me.

I started hoofing it down that mountain even faster, nervously looking behind me practically every other step. It doesn't take nearly as long to get down as it does to go up, and I was about halfway back down when I noticed something over to my right, about even with me, that didn't look good.

There was something black over there, and it was big, and it was paralleling me down the mountain. When I would stop to take a look behind me, it would stop, so that it was staying right even with me, but about say 100 yards away, just far enough that I really couldn't make out what it was, but I could tell how big it was in comparison to the juniper trees that spotted the mountainside. The thing was big, alright, really big.

Well, my first thought was how in the heck did a bi
black bear get out here, and why isn't it in hibernation.
That country is high desert, and the nearest bear country is
Black Mountain over east by the town of Craig, or the Uintas over in Utah to the northwest, but none of it less than 40
miles or so away, a long ways for a bear to hike.

My second thought was how long is that darn bear going to walk on its hind legs like that before it gets tired?
Bears walk on all fours.

My third thought wasn't a thought at all, it was more
an emotion. The thing had turned enough towards me and
was looking at me, and I could see it didn't have any fur on
its face, and what little I could make out of its face looked
awfully human.

The only consolation I had at that moment was that I
was only about a mile from my camp, and there was a fairly
deep gully between me and this thing. I knew because I
had tried to cut across that way, and it was deep enough I
didn't want to try it. It was also filled with snow which had
apparently avalanched down from the top some time ago,
probably after the last snowstorm we'd had.

I kept on going, and when I looked again, I was terrified—the thing was cutting over towards me, and it looked
like it had plenty of intent, like it knew I was there and was
planning an ambush or something. Why else would it be
cutting across towards me? And it looked really angry. Every once in awhile, it would stop and tear off a large branch
from a juniper tree and heave it towards me, even though it
wasn't close enough to reach me.

I would've stopped and kicked myself for not bringing my rifle, but I was in too much of a hurry.

Now this thing let out a shriek, and it chilled me to my bones. It didn't sound anything like before, like a woman screaming, but instead it sounded like a madman ready to murder someone. And I figured that someone was me.

The creature came to the gully and dropped down into it to cross. By then I wasn't really all that far away from it, and I knew this was my only chance, so I started running as fast as I could while it was down there and couldn't see me. Maybe I could get far enough down the hill that I would lose it. I was literally shaking, I was so terrified.

But then I heard what sounded like a rifle shot. Was one of the other guys out here on his day off and had seen the beast and was shooting at it? The odds of that were pretty slim, but my mind was trying to figure out why I had just heard a rifle shot.

Well, just then, I heard a roaring sound, and I knew what had happened. The beast had triggered an avalanche in the gully, and I could see a blue-white snow cloud rising up. It was a steep chute, and even without a lot of snow, it had the capacity to avalanche, which I then figured it did. But was the beast caught in it?

I wasn't going to stick around to find out. I can't tell you how fast I ran down that mountain, but it was record-breaking for me. I got to my tent and grabbed my rifle, then stood there by my truck and watched in the direction I'd just come.

Nothing. Nary a sound or sight of anything.

I was beside myself. Had I really seen this thing coming after me? Had I been drinking and forgot I'd been drinking? I just stood there, shaking, for the longest time, then I did something really stupid. I decided to go back and see what had happened.

I think having that rifle gave me more courage than I normally had, but I also think I needed to know what was going on to be able to stay there and sleep at night. I actually, in retrospect, would have been smarter to just pack up and leave right then, but that's never been one of my stronger department, brains.

So, I quickly made my way over to where the gully came down off the mountainside. I wanted to see up into it a ways, enough to figure out what was going on, so I kind of angled towards it. Well, I hadn't gone very far when I saw exactly what had happened.

This black thing had triggered an avalanche alright, and there he was, all hung up on the top of a small cliff, where a juniper tree brought down by the snow was wedged, the only thing keeping him from coming on off and falling a good forty feet or more, which I was sure would kill even a big guy like him.

Now keep in mind that now, today, I would call this a Bigfoot, but at the time, nobody in that part of the country had even heard of such a thing, so I had no idea what I was looking at. But no matter what it was, I had to feel a bit sorry for it. I could understand what it would feel like to be hung up there like that, just minutes from your death, and no idea what to do. That affected me, and like I said, he seemed almost human.

I just stood there watching, not sure what to do, when the most heart-rending moaning came out of this beast. You could tell he was frightened, and I figured he deserved what he got, since he was coming after me. But to leave him there, alone, to probably freeze to death or worse, to starve to death unless he got loose and fell first, was something I couldn't do. But yet, I had no idea how to help him, and even if I did, would he then come after me again?

Quite the quandary, but the problem solved itself, I'm happy to say. As I stood there watching, I noticed the sun went down over the horizon, and it suddenly got very cold. I don't know if that made the snow contract or something, but I could see a trickle of snow coming down the chute, and this soon turned into another small avalanche, which swept all around the creature as he hung on for dear life to the wedged tree. I was sure he would be swept over the edge.

The snow soon stopped, and he was still hanging there, but another tree had come down and wedged itself against the first tree. As I watched, this huge beast managed to twist himself around, using his arms and legs like a gorilla would, and pull himself up onto the second tree, which then gave him a means to leap to the edge of the gully. It was an athletic feat no human could have ever done, and he really did remind me of a giant monkey.

Well, I was glad to see him free, but now I was back to my original worries of whether or not he was going to come after me. I ran back over to my truck and got in, turning it around, ready to head out, but I could now see him running down the hill and to the west, away from me.

I sighed a sigh of relief, glad he'd lost interest. I sat there for a few minutes, watching to see if he would come back, then I got out, took down my tent, broke camp, then drove into Maybell, where I stayed at the motel each night until the job shut down.

The boys asked me why I'd moved into town, and I told them I was tired of being the first and last one at work every day. They laughed, and I never did tell them the truth. They wouldn't have believed me, anyway. I'm sure glad my daughter did when I told her years later.

And I will say that I carried that rifle with me on the loader every day and have never been as happy since to leave a place.

[2] Bone Games

. . . .

Jerry was a small wiry guy I met at a flyfishing class I was teaching in my home town. We got to talking afterwards, and when I learned he was camping in his little trailer, I invited him to come home with me for one of my wife Sarah's good home-made spaghetti dinners.

As we sat around after dinner, the talk inevitably turned to camping, and Jerry shared the following strange story. I've never heard anything like it, and I wondered if it were some kind of coming of age ritual.

I did get to meet his two cats, M&M, who he claims are way smarter than him, and this story makes you wonder. Nothing new there, animals seem to always beat us out when it comes to instinct, at least that's been my experience. Now if we could just learn to listen to them... —Rusty

My name is Jerry and I live in my RV full time. After I was laid off from my last job as a computer programmer, I sold my house and bought a little Casita travel trailer and a new Dodge pickup. I put a shell on the pickup and use the back for storing lots of water and supplies, and I can go some-times up to a month before I have to go to town for any-thing. I like to do what's called boondocking, which means you camp out with no hookups. I hate RV parks.

I have two cats, and I was trying to figure out how to make it so they could come along, as they're my buddies. I call them M&M for Max and Missy. They're both black and from the same litter when a friend's cat had kittens. I've had them since they were babies.

So, as things transpired, I taught them to walk on a leash, and I also built a wire cage off my trailer where they can go sit in the sun. They can go through a storage door and out into the cage, where they can sit and watch things happen. They love that little sunroom, and I just fold it up into the trailer when I travel.

Anyway, I usually spend two or three weeks in the same spot, going down to Arizona and New Mexico in the winter and then up further north in the summer. It's a really nice lifestyle, and I get computer internet jobs here and there. I don't need much money. I have a satellite dish that allows me to get the internet from pretty much anywhere. This all has some bearing on my story, so stick with me here.

OK, I was down in northern New Mexico, not too far from Taos, working my way north, as it was starting to get hot. I had driven up towards the ski area in the foothills of the Sangre de Cristo Mountains until I found a dirt road, then I just drove up it as far as I could go. I ended up in a small meadow in the trees, very quiet and peaceful and private, just my cup of tea.

Ah, the good life! I was stocked up and had every-thing I needed to stay awhile. People always ask me how I keep from getting bored out there in the same spot all the time, and I always say it's easy. I hike, listen to my satellite radio system, read lots of books on my Kindle, and do silversmithing. The silversmithing is starting to pay more than my programming, and I have several small galleries around the country who buy my stuff. So, I keep busy. And I also take M&M around for walks all the time on their leashes. I never get bored, and I never get lonely.

And I never get afraid—well, I didn't used to, anyway.

So, I pulled the trailer into this nice spot and unhooked the truck, got some things like my camp chair out, then set up the cat house. That's what I call the little wire room, the cat house.

I was busy messing around and finally went back inside to make some lunch, when I noticed M&M weren't in the cat house. That's usually the first thing they do, is run out into the cat house and sit there and survey their surroundings, like "Where we at now, Pops?"

They were both sitting by an open window, looking out, not wanting to go outside, just sitting there. That in itself should've told me something was up, as they'd never done this before, sit by a window when they could be in their cat house. I figured they were tired or something.

I made PBJ sandwiches and sat in my camp chair and ate, then made some tea. After a bit, I decided to take M&M for a little walk and see the country around camp. I went back inside and put their halters and leashes on them, then opened the door. Usually they'll bolt outside, as they love walks, but neither did, they just sat there. I tried to kind of drag them a little, but they started pulling back.

Neither wanted to go out of the trailer, which was another first.

This kind of made me stop and wonder if they weren't getting sick or something. This was worrisome, but they'd both eaten a good breakfast and acted fine otherwise, so I decided not to push it. Animals are just like us, they have their off days sometimes.

So, I grabbed my jacket and decided to go explore around camp a bit without them. They could sleep in the trailer. I set out a little pan of milk for them, then headed out, leaving the little meadow and following a small animal trail, walking into the aspen and fir forest.

It was a beautiful day, and I was pretty happy to be in such a nice spot. It felt private and sheltered, and the forest was pristine, unlike some of the areas I've been where people left trash and did ATV damage. I was soon in another small meadow, and as I crossed it, I noticed something white in a tree over on the north end. I decided to go see what it could be, as it was up there kind of high. I figured it was some trash that had blown in.

Well, when I got there, I could see there were about ten bones hung in this big pine tree, like ornaments on a Christmas tree. They were large bones, like from cattle. It was kind of weird seeing bones high in the tree as if someone had hung them up there, yet that someone would've had to be a lot taller than I was.

I stood there for awhile, trying to figure it out, when I started to feel uncomfortable. This was a first for me, as I usually feel much safer out in the woods than in town. I carry a knife in a case on my belt, but I've never had to use it for anything, and I've never felt the need to be armed.

The only thing out in the woods is an occasional bear and an even less occasional mountain lion, and I'd only seen one bear in all my camping times, so I didn't worry too much about wild animals.

But now, as I stood there, I felt uncomfortable, then I started to feel fear, which is another first for me. Like I said, I feel safer out there than in town.

I figured someone had been here before and found a cow skeleton and thrown it up in the tree for fun, but it seemed like the bones had been hung there. They just were too neat and all oriented the same way, and like I said, it would have to be someone real tall who could do that, like maybe eight or even nine feet tall. They just didn't look like they'd been thrown up there. Maybe someone had used a stick to somehow put the bones up there, I thought.

Well, the longer I stood there, the weirder I felt, so I just turned and hightailed it out of there, kind of looking back and all around me like maybe something was following me. It was that kind of feeling, like I wasn't alone, and I didn't like it one bit.

I got back to my little trailer and went inside, where the cats seemed awfully glad to see me, more so than usual. Now, keep in mind that while these things were happening, I wasn't paying attention to all these signs and putting them together, that came later when it was all over and I was thinking back. If I'd had the presence of mind to put this all together as it was happening, I would've been out of there immediately.

I sat there in my little trailer for a bit, kind of looking back the way I just came, wondering if there was a bear or something in there. That country only has black bears, so I wasn't too worried. I finally started feeling better and turned on the radio and started reading an old Western I'd picked up at the last laundromat. It was pretty good, and I got all involved in it and forgot about the weird feeling.

That evening was nice and cool, and there were no mosquitoes, something I really like about those dry New Mexico mountains. I sat out on my chair and drank tea, trying to coax the cats to come out into their cat house, but no go. They wanted nothing to do with being outside, and they actually acted like they wanted to hide. They kept trying to get into the cupboards and under the covers on my bed. In retrospect, animals have much better senses than we humans, and they pay attention to them.

Finally, the sun set and I decided to go to bed. I woke sometime in the middle of the night, which I sometimes do, and had to go take a leak. I stepped out of the trailer for a minute and did my thing in the bushes, and as I was standing there, I could hear a strange clanking kind of noise coming from the distance, the direction I'd found the bones. I went back to the trailer and stood in the door, listening.

It's hard to describe, but it sounded like a xylophone a little bit, like something hollow being hit with a hard stick. It was truly the strangest sound I've ever heard, and being out alone like that in the middle of nowhere made it even more unsettling. I listened until I started getting really freaked out, then I went back inside and locked the door. I decided that I would leave the next day. This place was just too strange.

I finally fell asleep and woke to the sun in my face. I'd slept way later than usual, but I still had a hard time waking up. After two cups of strong coffee and some oatmeal, I felt a little better and decided to try to get M&M to go out for a little walk with me. I was feeling different now that it was daylight and the strangeness of the night was gone.

But the cats wouldn't budge. In fact, neither of them had touched the canned food I'd given them as a treat, which was unheard of. I was now beginning to really worry they might be getting sick.

I decided to go ahead and hitch the trailer up, then I started putting things away. I would leave, but I wasn't in any real hurry, just sometime after lunch would do. I actually liked this spot a lot, and if it weren't for the strangeness, I would stay longer.

I got everything ready to go, then went inside and made some coffee and booted up my little laptop to check out nearby state parks, looking for the next spot.

Well, one of my main clients was a guy back east who owned a furniture supply company. He supplied stuff for schools, you know, desks and chairs and all that. I had built his online catalog and was the only one who really knew what the coding was all about.

There on my email was a message from him, and he was frantic. The entire thing had crashed, and he had several schools wanting to purchase stuff before their fiscal year ended. This crash was going to cost him big bucks if we didn't get it fixed immediately.

I sat down and got into it and finally solved the problem, but it wasn't until late afternoon. I really didn't want to take off in the evening with no idea where I was going. So, as you can probably guess, I was there for another night. I just hoped it wouldn't be like the previous night, though nothing had really happened, just the strange noises.

That evening, the cats seemed to be hungry, though they didn't eat much. But at least they were eating, so my worry about them being sick lessened. But there was still no way they wanted to go outside. I had taken their screen room down and closed up the trailer hole, which was really a door leading into the cargo area. I figured if things got too weird, we would just leave during the night, since everything was all packed and pretty much ready to go.

I sat out by the trailer after dinner, just looking at what I could see of the sunset through the trees and thinking about nothing much in general.

You know how there's usually a little breeze as the sun sets, as the sudden change in warmth changes the barometric pressure? Well, the evening breeze hit, but only for a moment, as it usually does, but this time it carried a strange odor on it. I tried to figure it out, but it wasn't quite the smell of a skunk, but close. It was more musky and foul smelling, and it also kind of smelled like something dead, all of that combined. The breeze died down and the smell went away.

I was again feeling some consternation. Maybe I should just get out now, while it was dusk and I could see a bit. But I hadn't really figured out where to go, and I didn't want to be going down the road in the dark, as it was rough. When you're pulling a trailer, even a small one, you kind of need a plan of where you're going to stop.

I was tired. I hadn't got enough sleep last night, and the intense work of the afternoon on the computer had helped wear me out. At least that's how I explain to myself later what I did, because there's no other explanation. It was a really stupid thing to do.

As I was taking my chair in, the noise from the previous night started up again. It was more distinct, and I think this was because the breeze was coming from that direction. It really didn't sound very far away at all. For the life of me, it sounded like bones whacking on bones.

Like I said, I was tired, and I just instinctively reacted. I decided to go see what it was. I closed the trailer door, made sure everything was ready to go, and checked that my keys were in my pocket, then slowly headed for the little meadow towards the direction of the sound. Something said to be extra cautious and to stay hidden, so I carefully kind of slinked from tree to tree. By now it was almost dark.

As I got closer, the smell started back up again, that skunky yucky smell. It was pretty gaggy at this point, but I kept going. The little meadow really wasn't that far from my camp, so it wasn't long until I was there, looking out from the edge of the trees. And sure enough, this was where the sound was coming from, and it was now pretty loud. Clank, clank, clank, it sounded just like bone on bone.

It took my eyes a minute to get used to the shadows, but I then stood there in a mixture of shock and fear. What I saw is hard to describe, but I'll try. It's partly hard to describe for two reasons: one, as soon as I realized what I was looking at, I ran, and two, my brain had trouble processing an image so foreign to it.

There, on the far side of the meadow where the bones had hung from the tree, were a dozen or so black masses—huge, thick, muscular, and terrifying black masses that stood upright, and several looked to be well over seven feet tall. It was now almost dark, so it was difficult to tell exactly what they looked like, but I could see well enough to make out general shapes.

They all had shaggy hair and walked on two legs with large muscular arms that were exceptionally long. They seemed to be a bit stooped at the shoulders with round heads that kind of came to a peak at the top. They looked like their heads kind of met their collar bones directly, without much of a neck.

As I stood there, a sense of terror washed over me that I've never felt before or since. I was downwind of them, and the smell was about to gag me, but what I saw puzzled me enough that I stood there for a few moments longer than I might have otherwise—they were doing something, and that something involved the bones that had been hanging in the tree, some kind of game or ritual or something.

One of them held a big bone, maybe a cow's leg bone, and one-by-one the others would come alongside him and try to knock the big bone from his hands with their own bones, which ranged from leg bones to collar bones, all the bones that had been hanging in the tree. It was maybe some kind of test of strength or something.

It was then I noticed a bunch of similar shadows, but smaller, sitting at the edge of the meadow across from me. This looked like a group of females and children, as they seemed to generally be a bit smaller, and the children ranged from small ones to what were probably teenagers. They sat there, watching this game or ritual or whatever it was.

I was only there for a moment, but as I stood there, one of the big guys managed to knock the leg bone from the other guy's hand. This was followed by a huge chattering from everyone, contestants and audience alike, and they sounded a lot like monkeys. Some of the females and children stood and started jumping up and down, and I swear to God they looked just like gorillas, at least their motions, anyway, though they were more like humans in their upright carriage. They were all very excited.

Now the guy who knocked the leg bone out of the big guy's hand, he and the big guy started wrestling while everyone stood around watching. It was something to behold, the strength and power of these animals, whatever they were. It was very scary, yet I couldn't take my eyes off them. I felt sick when I realized they could snap my neck in a heartbeat if one of them had wanted to.

I quickly came to my senses and snuck away, and when I was sure I was out of sight, I ran as hard as I could back to my trailer. I never let the cats ride free in the trailer, I always put them in the truck with me in their cat carriers, but that late evening, I simply jumped in my truck and headed out in the dark, cats still in the trailer. I didn't want to even turn on my headlights for fear the monsters would see me, but I had no choice, as it was now too dark to see without lights.

I drove out of there as fast as I could, and I think I put a few years on my rig, hitting ruts and bumps a bit faster than was prudent. It wasn't until I got back to the main highway that I stopped by the road, went and got the cats, and brought them into the cab with me. They were pretty shook up, to say the least, but not nearly as much as I was.

I drove on into Taos, gassed up, then headed north on the highway. I drove far into the night until I came to the Walmart in Durango, Colorado, then pulled into their parking lot. It was early in the morning, and I'd been on the road for hours. I was exhausted.

I took M&M into the trailer with me and fed them. They seemed really happy and ate like pigs. We all then crawled into my bed and I didn't wake up until mid-morning the next day when a big rig pulled in nearby.

I normally would never stay in a Walmart parking lot, but it felt so good to be there that I just stayed that day and into the next, resting and sleeping and trying to figure out what had happened. I finally called my son, who I knew would talk to me, as we're pretty close. After hearing my story, he told me I'd seen Bigfoot.

I would never have believed it if I hadn't seen it myself. And now I tend to camp more around people and not so much back in the woods alone. I just feel safer that way.

[3] The Hoaxer

· ·

This is a second-hand Bigfoot story, but I enjoyed it anyway. It was told over a campfire at Bear Lake, which isn't all that far from where it took place. The storyteller, Sandy, told me later that his friend Ryan is now a graduate student at Utah State, studying psychology, which for some reason seems appropriate.
—Rusty

I used to have a friend named Ryan, and we'd known each other since about third grade. We didn't really have much in common, to be honest, but we lived down the street from each other and were in the same grade, so we started walking home from school together and eventually became friends. Sort of a friendship of convenience, so to speak. We lived in Logan, Utah, which is on the lower slopes of the Bear River Mountains and the home of Utah State University.

I was kind of quiet and liked to read, and Ryan was loud and liked games and any kind of setting where he could make noise. Kind of like introverts and extroverts, I guess. Our friendship lasted until about high school, then it mostly ended. I got tired of Ryan's craziness and distanced myself from him.

You see, Ryan was what one would call a prankster. He seemed to really enjoy pulling pranks on people, and there was something in his personality that got off on it.

I used to think it was a power trip, that he was pulling something over on you so it made him feel powerful, but then I decided it was a superiority thing. Then later I found out he'd been teased and had lots of abuse from his older sister and brother, so I decided it was a form of vengeance, though on innocent people since he couldn't take it out on the original perpetrators.

Shoot, I'm no shrink, so maybe it was none of the above—or maybe all of the above. Who knows? I just knew he was starting to go where I didn't want to go with his pranks, and I quit hanging with him. He knew why, too, because I told him, and I'd told him many times he was going too far with things, but he never believed me.

But something interesting happened later that cured Ryan of pranks, and I think after that, Ryan maybe did believe me that pranks could lead to pain, whether mental or physical, and they weren't really a good thing to engage in.

Ryan was playing jokes on people the day I met him. In fact, that's how I met him—he had just moved to the neighborhood and was walking home from school. He was dragging along like he could barely walk, and when he saw me, he introduced himself and asked if I would help him get home, as he was having trouble.

I asked him what was wrong, and he said he hadn't been out of surgery very long and had a lung removed because of some infection. Could I help him? He was pleading, and of course, who wouldn't help? I carried his books and let him kind of lean against me until we got to his house, then he said thanks and went inside.

Next day, he was fine and seemed to have forgotten all about having had a lung removed when we were all playing soccer. I asked him how he was doing, and he acted like he didn't know what I was talking about, then when he remembered, he said he'd had a miraculous recovery. I think he was a pathological liar on top of being a prankster, and the two kind of went together.

Anyway, he was always pulling stunts like that. One time, he talked me into helping him drag some old straw bales down to an irrigation canal, where we cut off the string and set the bales on fire. They went merrily floating down the canal all ablaze, ending up coming aground at some old guy's yard and setting his weeds on fire. The fire department came and put it out, and nobody ever knew what had started it—except me and Ryan, that is.

Another time, we spent all day collecting tumbleweeds from a nearby field and stacking them in an empty lot at the edge of town. That pile was a good twenty feet high. When the winds came up, those weeds blew all over town, which we thought was pretty funny.

Well, when a kid's in grade school, you can see pulling a few pranks and such, as it's just part of what makes kids kids, especially boys. But when they get older, you expect them to outgrow it. The ones that don't sometimes end up in jail.

Ryan's pranks were pretty harmless, except for a couple like the straw bale incident. Most of his pranks would typically serve to embarrass someone, and it was never Ryan who was embarrassed, guaranteed. And when Ryan got into middle school, instead of outgrowing it, he just got worse.

For example, there was the time he talked some younger kid into helping him steal some chickens. That in itself was bad enough, but the purpose of stealing the chickens was to put them in the school principal's office, where they ended up pretty much destroying the place. I think he got that one from reading about some senior class pranks.

Ryan had pried the window open and tossed these poor birds in there, and they weren't found until the next day. He never got caught, but I found out about it later and really wanted to turn him in but couldn't do it, as we were supposed to be friends. But I thought it was a pretty crappy thing to do and told him so. That was one incident that made me question our friendship.

Ryan wasn't dishonest overall, though he could tell lies with the best of them, but he never cheated on tests or anything like that. He seemed to have his own set of standards, and they always revolved around pranking other people. If it were necessary for a good prank, sure he would lie and steal, but if not, he was as honest and trustworthy as they came. I often wondered if he could see the cognitive dissonance in his own actions.

Did he ever get caught? Sure, but what do you do? I think he may have been in a couple of fights a time or two, but nothing very serious, and it sure didn't slow him down.

He usually didn't do anything illegal, except for the chickens and the straw bales, so nobody with any authority was ever after him. And he was amazingly good at talking you out of being mad.

He did get suspended once for three days in middle school for disassembling the teacher's desk, the one she always pounded on when yelling at the students to quiet down, which then went flying all over the room the next time she pounded on it. That was one of the few pranks where he actually had an appreciative audience. And he also was kicked out of the Boy Scouts for duct taping the zippers of everyone's tents closed with them inside sleeping, which he claimed he didn't do.

That was the one thing that really bummed him out, because I think he really liked the Boy Scouts and wanted to stay in it. By then, Ryan had earned himself a reputation, so he naturally got blamed, since his tent was the only one not taped shut. He said it was a setup to make him look guilty. He was guilty, if not of that prank, of plenty of others.

Well, fast forward to high school. In spite of his usual stuff of setting classroom clocks forward ten minutes and nonsense like that, he did pretty good at staying out of trouble.

Until he found out the Boy Scouts were having a big campout in nearby Spring Hollow Campground, where he ended up getting himself into a situation that ended his pranking for good, a situation he never forgot.

Now, Boy Scouting is really big in Utah. There are lots of scout troops, as the main church there has really embraced the program, and there's always something going on in the scouting world.

You can easily spot Utah Boy Scouts, as they always have Springbar tents, which are made in Salt Lake City. Some of those tents have been in the scout business longer than the scout leaders, forty years or more.

Well, one day I got a call from Ryan, asking me to come over to his house to see something he'd built, as he wanted my opinion. At this point, we weren't talking much, and I felt kind of guilty, I guess, so I went on over there, half expecting to be pranked.

He took me down to his basement, where he had something big hidden under a sheet, something that was about six feet tall and four feet wide.

He pulled the sheet off, and I couldn't believe my eyes—it was a life-sized Bigfoot, or at least how I would picture a life-sized Bigfoot would look, as I'd never actually seen one.

I examined it, and he'd made it out of stiff cardboard on a light wood frame, then painted it. It looked pretty real, with long dark hair and red eyes and a snarl and teeth that would scare one to death if you saw it at night. I asked him what it was for, and he said he was going to make a Bigfoot movie.

I was impressed and said so. Ryan then took out his iPod, and out of it came the scariest howling I've ever heard.

"What the heck is that?" I asked.

"Bigfoot sounds from the internet. It goes with the movie. I'm going to put it on my boombox so I can blast it out in the woods."

We talked a little about his movie, then, Ryan being who he was, asked me to help him get the Bigfoot out of his basement. Of course, he had neglected to tell me that was his main purpose for asking me over, but I didn't mind, and we angled the thing out and took it out to his garage. It wasn't heavy, just bulky.

I thought the movie would be fun, but I really didn't want to get involved, so I wished him luck with it and went home. Of course, he may have been planning on making a movie, but he was also planning on using it for something else, which he neglected to mention. Good old Ryan.

Well, Spring Hollow Campground is about four miles up Logan Canyon from town, and a really nice place to camp with a wetlands nearby with lots of cattails, willows, and birds. The local scout troop would be camping there for the weekend over in one of the group sites.

I think Ryan still held a grudge against the scout leader who'd given him the boot, and that scout leader would be there with his troop. I found all this out later, of course.

Apparently Ryan was able to carry this Bigfoot guy on his back, having rigged a sling. He then managed to get it onto his dirt bike and ride up the canyon real slow, and I guess a couple of times the thing almost took off with him, like a big sail.

He did this at night, of course, and took it up behind where the scouts were camped, into the trees and set it up, making sure it was in their line of sight through the thick trees. He then got his boombox and set it next to the Bigfoot. He then bided his time, sitting there in the dark, watching the festivities around a big bonfire.

This is one time I kind of felt sorry for Ryan when I heard about it later, as I knew he felt like he'd been cheated out of being in Boy Scouts. The tent incident had made him feel the pain of being pranked, which was ironic, as it was the very same thing he'd done numerous times to others.

So, he sat there, and when it started getting late and the kids were winding down a bit, he picked up a big piece of wood and started knocking on a tree with it.

Wham! Wham! Wham! Three times, then he'd stop. It took awhile before he got any kind of response, but soon it quieted down around the fire. He did it again, and soon one of the kids was answering him back, knocking on a tree by the camp.

The plan was for him to get their attention, and then they would shine their lights into the trees and see the Bigfoot and be terrified. He would hide in the bushes and enjoy it all while blasting out the howling on his boombox.

But so far, nobody seemed very scared. They acted like they enjoyed the idea of a Bigfoot being out there. There were now several of them tree knocking.

He started whacking on the tree again, and the kids answered. This went on several times, but one time, when Ryan stopped, he swore he could hear knocking in the woods up the steep canyon way behind him. Logan Canyon cuts through the rugged mountains, with lots of big rocks and thick stands of timber.

Ryan at first thought someone up the canyon was mimicking his wood knocking, so he just continued on with his prank. The kids below were now getting more worked up, which is exactly what he wanted.

Now it was time for the recording. Hopefully, someone would shine a light over to where the Bigfoot was and they would all freak out. He'd placed it not too far from camp, but not close enough that anyone would have the nerve to go see what it was up close.

He cranked up the sound recording, which had a really powerful bass. Now he was having fun, as the kids were yelling and some were running and getting into the scout vehicle. The scout leader was now walking around looking distressed and trying to calm the kids down.

Ryan was rolling over, laughing hard. He could hear just enough to make out bits and parts of the conversations. One of the kids was yelling, "We gotta get outta here!" over and over, scared to death.

Sure enough, someone pointed a big flashlight in the direction of the sound and apparently saw Ryan's Bigfoot, because this started a whole new round of yelling and screaming.

Ryan's prank was working, and he was about to pee himself, he was having so much fun.

But suddenly, he could hear a thumping behind him, and it was so loud it made the ground shake. Ryan suddenly felt the hair on his neck stand up and his stomach begin to feel queasy from a stench that came from the thick oak and maple woods behind him.

He turned around just in time to see a large tree come hurtling towards him, barely missing his head and crashing into the Bigfoot cutout. Then he saw what had thrown the tree, and he started screaming, which of course added to the fears below, but which wasn't supposed to be part of the prank.

Even though it was dark, Ryan got a close-up look at a real Bigfoot, and he described it as being around seven to eight feet tall and weighing about 600 pounds. What he could see of its face was like an ape's, though longer and with no hair around the eyes nor on the cheeks, where its skin was chocolate colored. It had a very prominent brow, and dark eyes that seemed to glow.

Ryan turned and ran towards the camp, still screaming. As he came bounding through the brush and rocks, he tripped and fell, then got up again just as a rock came hurtling behind him, barely missing him.

As Ryan came screaming into camp, the scouts crammed close to the fire for safety, while the leader shone a flashlight Ryan's way, which of course made it harder for him to see where he was going. But he finally made it into the fire circle, where he collapsed, sobbing.

Now the Bigfoot let out a howl like nothing any of them had ever heard, and sounds of shattering wood filled the forest. A tree came flying their way, a big one, freshly wrenched from the ground, but didn't quite make it to the fire circle.

At this point, the scout master decided it would be prudent to get everyone into the van and out of there, so he did, including Ryan, and left the campground, Springbar tents and gear and the fire burning. They were soon back in Logan, where he dropped Ryan off at his house, then took all the kids home.

The next day, Ryan's mom took him back for his dirt bike. He hadn't said a word to her about his hoax, and instead had made up a story about not wanting to ride it

back down to town in the dark. The scouts eventually re-
trieved their gear, and that was the end of that camping
trip, though it wasn't the end of the talk about Bigfoot.

After I heard about all this from Ryan, he talked me into
going back up there to get his little portable boom box. I
reluctantly did, and we climbed up into the trees above the
campground, where we found it right where he'd left it.
Not far away was the Bigfoot cutout, torn to shreds.

We didn't stay long, and I noticed that Ryan was very
subdued. Not long after, he was invited to a scout meeting
to relate his story to the scouts, which of course was quite
different from what had actually happened. He told me
later that he'd been invited to be a scout assistant.

Since this was the same leader who had kicked him out,
Ryan was very honored and jumped at the chance. He'd become kind of a hero to everyone, in spite of his blubbering
and screaming that night.

I would suspect he made a good leader and came up
with some very creative things for them to do, and I know
that he didn't allow any pranks.

[4] Just Winging It

· ·

I've never considered flyfishing to be an extreme sport, except maybe for the bit of excitement when you hook a nice big Brookie or Rainbow, and that can get interesting. So when a fellow named Jeff joined one of my guided trips, I just figured he was another of the mellow souls that frequent my career as a fishing guide.

Turns out he used to be an adrenaline junkie, and this story pretty much exemplifies a unique way to get one's thrills. Jeff told it over a nice campfire out by the Williams Fork River in northwest Colorado, one of my favorite fishing areas, and one that figures in a later story in this book. Jeff's adventure must have been enough for one lifetime, because he afterwards took up the Zen sport of flyfishing and seemed quite happy to do so. —Rusty

I used to be a hang glider pilot, and all my free time was spent pursuing this sport. Sometimes, when the bug bit, I would even do it on my not-so-free time, too, like when I was supposed to be working and would just call in sick. That's how it is when you're an adrenaline junkie, nothing stands in the way of your thrills, and hang gliding was pretty much an adrenaline rush if anything was—especially where I practiced my art, which was high above Telluride, Colorado.

I was a member of what's called the Telluride Airforce, a local hang gliding and paragliding club there. Our main launch was at Gold Hill, at the top of the Telluride Ski Area, at a mere 12,250 feet. We would land in town, at around 8750 feet. The valley is surrounded by huge mountains, which are in turn surrounded by more huge mountains, on and on as far as the eye can see.

So, hang gliding in Telluride is not for the faint of heart, and the tricky air currents make things even more interesting. I lived there five years, and spent most of my free time flying, so maybe you'll understand where I was coming from when I tell the rest of this story. I would also take trips when I could and go fly places like Yosemite, which is totally crazy with its huge granite walls. I was considered a pretty expert glider by myself, though some of my friends said I took too many risks.

Time moves on, and I had to leave Telluride, as my girlfriend kicked me out, and she was the one with the money and thereby the house. In retrospect, I kind of blew a good thing and should've spent more time with her instead of flying, but oh well, hindsight's 20-20, as they say. I became a bachelor again because of my obsession with flying.

So, picture a guy in his late 20's, in the throes of heartbreak, without much of a job (I worked on a snowcat in the winter grooming the ski area trails and worked part-time as a furniture mover in the summer). I didn't have enough money to rent a place, not in pricey Telluride, so, I hit the road.

I figured now was my chance to go fly a few places I'd been wanting to see, and then I would have to find work. I had a cousin in Tucson who said I could come stay with her for a bit and help her remodel her house, so I decided to head south, taking my time, hitting up some places I wanted to go see on the way.

I had an old Jeep Cherokee that I'd built a rack on to carry my wing, and I had camping gear, so all I needed for my trip was gas money and some food. I had a few dollars saved up, so I wasn't too worried about anything—I would just take it easy and have fun, try to forget my problems. At least I didn't own much of anything, so I was pretty footloose. My wing and gear were worth maybe three grand at most, and my Jeep maybe another three grand. That was the sum total of my assets, and, unbeknownst to me, that would soon be cut in half.

My first stop was a bit west instead of south, but I had always wanted to fly that area around Canyonlands National Park in Utah. So I made it to the Moab area, all excited about taking off from the Island in the Sky and soaring down into the deep canyons. I drove up on the Island and set up camp for the night, but the next morning the weather was bad, as a big low front had come in from the west.

I drove back into town and checked out the forecast. It was supposed to be bad for the next several days, so I decided to head south after all. I would go on down to Zion National Park, which looked to be too far south for this storm. I'd always wanted to fly down there.

Now, in my own defense, let me say that since I'd flown in Yosemite, where it's legal, I thought it was OK to fly in any national park. I found out later that Yosemite is the only one where it is legal, but that's getting ahead of myself a bit.

I headed south, spending some time in Capitol Reef and Bryce, just hiking and being lazy. After a few days, I finally arrived at the east entrance of Zion, and all the way over to the main part of the park, I was scouting out takeoff sites.

The east entrance is over by Mt. Carmel Junction and what I would call the upland side of the park, more of a highland area than the west entrance, with a number of old roads going up onto the mesas. The mesas are cut by a number of narrow canyons, like the one with the Zion Narrows and the famous slot canyon called the Subway.

I came to the park headquarters and was very disappointed when I was told you had to ride a shuttle bus to see the main part of Zion, where the Great White Throne, Angel's Landing, and all the big landmarks were. No private vehicles.

This kind of irritated me, I guess, partly since I was already in a bad frame of mind from splitting up with my girlfriend. I was really angry deep inside, as she'd done me wrong, going out with a good friend, or what used to be a good friend. So what if I'd never been around, she still did me wrong, and I felt cheated.

So, instead of just getting on the shuttle bus, I decided I would see the park my own way on my own terms. I went back the way I came, back through the tunnels that cut through the huge cliffs when you come in from the east.

I went back to Mt. Carmel and bought a topo map and some lunch, then went and studied the map in a big grassy park near the store. I then headed back towards Zion, but took an old road that the map showed going out on some mesa and ending at the edge of a canyon.

It took awhile to get there, but when I arrived, it was a stupendous place. The road stopped in a small clearing right smack on the edge of a huge canyon, and it was pretty heady. By then, it was getting late, so I pulled out my little tent and made camp, watching an incredible sunset of reds and even greens at the end.

I slept well, and the next morning I decided to go ahead with my plan. My map showed this canyon eventually draining down into the main part of the park, and I could make out what looked like a good meadow to land in, not far from the highway.

One should always do a visual of where they're going to land before taking off, and I had no proof if that meadow would be a good landing spot. I would never be that stupid now, but like I said, I wasn't in a very good frame of mind. I was being foolish and reckless, and it's kind of a miracle I didn't get killed, all in all. I might add at this point that I no longer fly, since I don't have a wing anymore.

OK, so I got up, had some breakfast, paced around a bit, then went for it. I assembled the wing and harness and finally stood there, ready, at the edge of the cliffs. My plan was to land down in the park, hitch a ride back up the highway to where the road cuts off, then walk to my Jeep, which was maybe two or three miles up this back road, then go back for the wing.

If I were lucky, I could maybe pull off a two or three hour flight, see Zion like nobody on foot ever could, then be back up here before dark and go get my wing. That was the plan.

I knew I was in for some extreme flying, as the air currents in big canyons like this can be really unpredictable. You get updrafts and downdrafts when least expected. If I were lucky, I'd get caught in a big elevator, which is a big smooth thermal that can take you up for a long ways. I stood there and watched a pair of ravens riding the updrafts and then went and scouted where I wanted to do my cliff launch.

Every time I take off, it's the most incredible feeling. It's hard to describe. Of course, taking off and landing are the most dangerous parts, but taking off of a cliff can be pretty crazy. I got a running start and just launched off the edge of that big cliff. Cliff launches can be dangerous, as your wing can turn on you and not get any loft if you twist when you come off the cliff. Then it's all over.

Well, this is actually what almost happened, and I thought for a minute I was a goner. But I managed to get some lift going, and just as I did, I realized I was about to crash into the far side of the canyon, so I turned hard and barely cleared the cliffs. This was enough to wake me up a bit from my mad rush to kill myself, because I had a pretty good surge of fear—not adrenaline, just pure fear. And all of a sudden, I wanted to live.

I soared down through the canyon, and gradually the fear subsided and was replaced by the awe that I always feel when flying. And to be flying in Zion! I caught a nice updraft and came out of the canyon and up over the high-lands.

I flew for awhile, enjoying the views, then spotted another canyon below me, which I figured was the Narrows, from studying my map earlier. I really wanted to fly over it. It's a pretty famous part of Zion, a slot canyon that can be really dangerous if it flash floods. I banked over it, then went lower so I could see down into its dark depths.

Before I knew it, I was in the canyon, flying with barely enough room between my wingtips to clear the walls. I guess my fear of death had gone away and the bravado was back, because all I felt was exhilaration. I heard some hikers yelling up at me, then barely pulled up in time to avoid hitting the walls, as the canyon narrowed.

Anyway, I could go on and on, but the upshot was that I had an amazing flight, and I had also managed to attract the attention of the park rangers, though I didn't know it, who had called the local sheriff to assist in my arrest when I landed. I think they figured I was going to come down there near park headquarters.

I was pretty lost at this point and had no idea where that little landing meadow on my map was. I didn't even know which drainage I was in until, sure enough, I spotted park headquarters not far below. Now remember, I didn't really think I was doing anything illegal at the time, so I decided to see if I could find a place to land down there.

I scoped it out, and when I saw a park ranger waving at me, I waved back. I circled, thinking I could land in a back parking lot that was almost empty, but when I came back over, the ranger started yelling at me and then got into his car and turned on the siren.

Uh oh, maybe I was in trouble, I thought, so I pulled up and tried for some altitude. I needed a different place to land. I soared higher and higher, catching a thermal, until the park headquarters was a tiny building far below.

I noticed that the air currents had changed, and it occurred to me that maybe I could fly right back to where I'd taken off, so I banked in that direction. That would be handy.

But now I was totally lost. There are a number of big drainages coming into the park, and I had no idea which one was my canyon. I tried to head back to the highway and use it for a landmark, but now it was gone, too. Somehow I was all turned around. I hadn't bothered to even use my GPS.

I'd been up for several hours at this point, and I was starting to get tired. I was ready to land. These uplands are heavily timbered with thick stands of juniper and pinyon trees and even ponderosa pines at the higher elevations, and I was now above timber and could see no place to come down. Man, I was so disoriented.

I finally spotted an old dirt road below me and decided that was good enough. I would land and walk back to the highway, then figure out where my Jeep was and take it from there. I had to do something soon, as the day was wearing on and I was getting further and further out into the wilderness.

I circled and circled down until I was finally in a position to land on the road, then I came on down. I hadn't counted on the road being so rutted, and as I landed, I did a ground loop, coming down with one foot in the rut and one on the flat road. I then did a major face plant, my wing coming down hard on top of me, messing up the landing wires.

I just lay there for awhile in intense pain, wondering what I'd broken. It took me maybe ten minutes before I even felt like trying to get up. I just lay there, moaning in pain, thinking I'd broken my ankle where I'd twisted it in the rut.

But all of a sudden, I got real quiet, because someone was standing directly over me. I thought maybe I was dying and hallucinating and it was an angel or something.

But it would have to be a really big angel, a dark angel, because it was all black. Maybe I'd landed in the place I didn't want to be instead of heaven. Yikes. Anyway, that's what my brain was saying, trying to process what this big black thing standing over me could be. I quit moaning and just lay there, real still.

Now my brain said I was in big trouble. I could barely move, and this had to be a big bear standing looking at me. I had to do something before it attacked, as I was in a very vulnerable position, just laying there. I twisted myself around into a sitting position, bumping against my wing so it moved a bit.

This seemed to scare the bear, which jumped back a little. I slowly unhooked my harness. My bag was still around me, this thing you wear and tuck your legs up into when flying. I stood up, and it trailed behind me like the stinger end of a wasp. It probably looked really weird, but I've heard that one should try to look big and bad when encountering a bear, so I figured the suit would increase my size.

Now I realized I had probably sprained my ankle. I stood there, leaning against the frame of my wing, wondering what in the hell I was going to do. There was no way I could walk out, and nobody knew where I was. And to make things worse, there was this huge bear not far away.

As I stood there and my mind cleared a bit, I began to realize that what I was looking at was no bear. It was bigger and bulkier than any bear I'd ever seen, and it had what looked to be long thick hair, not fur, hair like a human, but all over its body. And its arms where exceptionally long. The shoulders were thick and strong looking, and it didn't appear to have a neck.

We both just stood there, looking at each other. It had huge eyes that were liquid looking, with no whites, and seemed very intelligent. In retrospect, this thing was probably as shocked as I was, seeing this weird creature come down from the sky and land nearby, a creature that looked like a human but had giant wings that it could remove.

I can't say I wasn't scared, in fact, I was terrified. But I didn't know what to do, so I started quietly talking to it, saying stuff like, "Hey, big fellow, whatcha doing out here in the woods, shouldn't you be in the zoo?" Crazy stuff like that. But it just stood there.

I now tried to put some weight on my ankle, and sure enough, it felt like a bad sprain. I was totally screwed. Maybe this big animal thing could help me, I thought, then realized how desperate I must be to even think such a thing, as it was more likely to eat me.

It then dawned on me what I was talking to. It had to be a Bigfoot. I didn't know much about Bigfoot, having never seen one before, but I remembered a few stories I'd heard that said Bigfoot was territorial and wouldn't harm you if you left its territory. I had to get out of there, but how?

Now, the strangest thing happened. This creature turned a bit sideways, and I could now tell it was a female because it had breasts. And just then, she looked into the trees near the clearing I'd landed in and began making a chattering sound, just like a very large monkey. And what really terrified me was the fact that the chattering was answered from the trees. She stepped back and walked to the forest, where she just blended in with the foliage.

There was more than one of these things around! I kicked out of the rest of the harness, then sank back down, half sitting on the frame of my wing, feeling terrified and defeated. There was absolutely nothing I could do but accept my fate. Maybe she'd lost interest and would leave me alone.

My ankle was now starting to throb. I involuntarily let out a moan. I had really done a number on it. It was late-afternoon by now, and even though it was summer and the days were long, there was no way I could walk what was surely several miles to the highway, let alone before dark.

But now I could see something coming back out of the trees. Holy crap! There were now two of them, and they were coming over to where I was. I wanted to run, but I couldn't even walk, so I just sat there, about ready to pee my pants. That was when I saw that the female was carrying a young one.

The second Bigfoot must be her mate, I figured, as it was much larger and even more muscular. Seeing the male made me want to start blubbering, he was so massive and terrifying. He could kill me with one blow, and here they came.

But they seemed curious, not angry. The male walked over to me and the wing and just stood there, looking at me. I now wanted to appear even smaller so he wouldn't see me as a threat, but I later thought how silly that was, because compared to him, I was already like a gnat. So I just leaned there on the frame and tried to avoid eye contact, looking down towards the ground.

He slowly came right up to me, but he wasn't interested in me at all. He wanted to examine the wing. He very gingerly reached out and touched it like it was a trap and he was ready to jump back. Once he figured out it was inanimate, the female came over to also examine it, holding her baby on her hip. The baby Bigfoot sure did eye me, and I finally looked up and smiled at it. I figured I was a goner anyway, so I was beginning to not care.

The little kid or whatever you would call it smiled back, its square teeth showing! And now the mom and dad noticed and seemed to relax. They were now right next to me. People have asked me if they smelled bad, and I have to say no, they really didn't, just kind of mildly like wet dogs. Maybe Bigfoot has some kind of glands like a skunk it can activate when it wants, but these guys were fine.

I have to admit I wasn't feeling very sociable. I noticed a large stick on the ground nearby, and I slowly kind of hopped over and picked it up. By now, the throbbing wasn't quite as bad, but there was still no way I was going much of anywhere. But I had to put some distance between me and this family in case they changed their mind and decided I was a threat.

I used the stick as a sort of crutch and hopped a bit away to a large rock, where I sat down for a minute, then hopped away a bit further. They were keeping an eye on me, but were also rather enthralled with the wing, and the mom had already managed to rip a piece of the nylon off. This gave me pause, as that was thick and tough nylon that I would need a good industrial pair of scissors to cut. Yow, scary. At this point, they could have it, I just wanted out of there.

I kept hopping down the road, using the stick as a crutch, then realized there were fresh vehicle tracks in the dirt, and they appeared to be going towards the edge of the mesa, not back towards the highway. It then dawned on me that maybe, just maybe, I was on the same road I'd driven up last night. Maybe my Jeep wasn't all that far away.

Should I go back up the road or try to somehow get to the highway? What if it wasn't my vehicle? At this point, it didn't matter, if it was just another human being I'd be happy. And from the way the cliffs angled back, I knew the road had to end not too far ahead.

I knew that sooner or later the Bigfoot would get tired of the novelty of the wing and maybe come looking for me. The thought sent a chill up my back. My ankle was burning hot, and I could see it was swelling up. I sat down on a rock for a minute and took off my shoe and sock.

I couldn't go very far without resting, but I finally managed to get up the road far enough that I felt better, as the Bigfoot didn't seem to be following me, not yet, anyway.

Well, I won't go into how long it took me, how scared I was, and how I at one point just sat down and cried, both from the pain and fear and from feeling abandoned by my girlfriend, but it was almost dark when I reached the end of the road, and sure enough, there sat my Jeep. I just crawled into it and cried in relief.

But I then discovered that I couldn't drive, as my ankle was so messed up, and I needed both feet, one for the clutch and the other for the gas. But using the stick I'd been carrying, I managed to put it in first, and that's how I drove out, in first gear, all the way. It took me quite a while to get to the highway, and the whole time I wondered if I were going to be attacked by Bigfoot.

I then managed to get the Jeep into third and drove on back to a motel at Mt. Carmel, where I hobbled inside and got a room. I then crashed hard, once again feeling like crying, but now because I'd survived.

I never went back for the wing. I stayed two days in that motel, waiting for my ankle to get better, then I drove back through Zion, as I wanted to get on the freeway west of the park.

As I stopped at the park entry booth, a ranger came out and asked me about the rack on my Jeep. He asked if I knew anyone who had been flying a hang glider in the park recently. Apparently, they had sent a couple of rangers out to find this guy, but he had just disappeared.

I lied through my teeth and smiled and said no, that I had bought the Jeep with the rack and had no idea what it was for.

They waved me on by, then I drove on through Springdale, the little park town there, then eventually on over to Toquerville and got on I-80. I turned south and never looked back, headed for Tucson.

[5] Gorilla Gulch

· ·

I've always been fascinated by place names, as they can tell you a lot about an area and what the early people found there. And places with names that have the words devil, spirit, and gorilla are, in my mind, possible Bigfoot territory.

So, when a fellow named Pete told this story over a campfire not far from the Elk River in northwest Colorado, it made me want to go over into central Utah and see what Gorilla Gulch was all about—well, go in theory, anyway. —Rusty

My buddies and I used to be avid ATVers and loved taking our off-road vehicles out to explore new places. I've since kind of lost interest and would rather be standing by some nice stream fishing with nary a care. But when I was younger, I really enjoyed getting out like that.

At the time, I lived in Salt Lake City, and it's a rat race, so every chance I could get, I liked to head out and get into the back country. When I was just getting started, we would stay in RV parks and just do day rides, but after awhile, you don't want to have to come back and retrace your route, so

I started carrying a tent and gear on my ATV and spending a night or two out. It's kind of like backpacking, in that you can't take a ton of stuff, but it's a lot easier (and noisier, I might add).

At the time this happened, the Paiute ATV Trail was just getting started, and my buddy Carl and I decided to go down and give it a look. I'm not sure whose idea the trail was, but I'm pretty sure it was a coordinated effort by the communities of central Utah to try and drum up some tourism business.

They took a bunch of old trails and mining roads and figured out how to connect them into one big trail that would go through their communities and then called it the Paiute Trail. ATVers like it because they know they're welcome, and it's a good way to connect with other ATVers. The Paiute Trail has maps with descriptions, too, so you know what the trails are like and what to expect.

Anyway, not to get into all that, but my buddy and I decided to go down to the little town of Marysvale, which is just down the road from the Big Rock Candy Mountain, if you've ever heard of that. There's a nice RV park there that caters to ATVers, and you can leave your truck and trailer and ride the trail as long and as far as you want—the trail is over 900 miles long. We wanted to ride up into the portion that goes into the Tusher Mountains, as we'd never been there.

The Tushers are pretty much off the beaten path, and most people don't even know they exist. They're volcanic and rise to around 12,000 feet, marking the boundary between the Great Basin and the Colorado Plateau. They're rugged and really beautiful, but also very inaccessible, except for some old mining and jeep roads.

They're used some by cattlemen for grazing, but you almost never see anyone hiking or camping there, at least not when we were there. I think this is mostly because they're not close to any cities—or even towns, for that matter.

Anyway, off we went to the Tushers and the Paiute Trail. We loaded up the ATVs on my trailer and headed down to Marysvale, which isn't much of a town at all, just a few hundred or so people. We spent our first night at the RV park in our tents, then headed out the next morning on the Paiute Trail, which you can ride to straight out of the RV park, which was nice.

We headed west and were soon going out of town on a forest road up Beaver Creek, where there were lots of cottonwoods and willows. Before long, we were in a pinyon and juniper forest, and then the road quickly climbed up into spruce and fir. We were soon at another junction, where we headed south, deep into the heart of the Tushers—and deep into a wild country that had inhabitants we had never heard of.

After the incident I'm about to recount occurred and we were back home, I found an old historic map of the area that had a name not on our newer map: Gorilla Gulch. If you ask anyone in the area about Gorilla Gulch, they'll probably just laugh, assuming they've even heard of it. But ask an oldtimer and you'll get a different reaction, because there's a reason it was called that. We discovered that reason, and I believe the original inhabitants of the gulch were at one time more plentiful.

Two months after all this happened, I went back down there and asked around. One old rancher knew exactly what I was talking about, and he really didn't want to be quoted, but he told me most everybody that knew anything avoided that area like the plague.

Well, unbeknownst to us, we were heading straight toward it.

It was getting late, so we found a nice spot not far off the road and set up camp. It was great being outdoors, and the September weather was perfect, though a bit chilly at night up in the high country. We had a great dinner, built a fire, and really enjoyed being out. I slept like a baby in my little camp tent, a little Coleman dome.

The next day, we went further into the backcountry, higher into the Tushers. We met a few other ATVers, but pretty much had the place to ourselves, at least until night hit. And I will say that our visitor that night turned us both into religious men, at least temporarily.

It was getting on towards evening, and we found a little dirt road that wound up into a small valley and decided to go on up it and see if we could find a good camp spot. The road wound along a small stream that was flanked by aspens and wild rose. We finally came to a little meadow that would make the perfect camp, and we stopped for the night and unloaded our gear.

After setting up our little tents and laying out our sleeping bags, we set to collecting wood for a fire. We had bought some really nice thick steaks and were looking forward to having them for dinner. It wasn't long until we had a nice fire going and steaks cooking on a grill.

I kicked back against a rock and watched the last rays of sunset disappear into a red sky. It looked like we were maybe in for a weather change, but the forecast had been good, so I wasn't too worried. We were only going to be out one more night after that one. We were happy campers.

If you've ever camped, you know the feeling of complete freedom and contentment you get when the day is done, camp's all tidy, and dinner's cooking over an open fire.

The steaks took awhile to cook, and in retrospect, I think the smell may have been what attracted our unexpected guest, though he came in too late for dinner.

We talked about all those things you talk about around a campfire, and after the steaks were ready, we both sat in silence eating and watching as the night sky unfolded its millions of stars. There's nothing like the stars in the clear sky of the Tushers. You feel like you could just reach up there and touch them.

Well, after dinner, we sat and talked awhile longer and smoked cigars, something we didn't get to do at home (wives, and that's all I'll say about that, ha). We were tired, so we were about ready to call it a day, when Carl, who was leaning against a rock staring into the fire, sat straight up. I was in the middle of saying something, and he held his hand up like you do when you want someone to stop.

I shut up and listened, but didn't hear a thing.

"What was it?" I whispered, but just then, I got my answer.

Deep in the distance, and I mean deep, as if miles away, came a howling sound. You could tell that whatever was making it was really big and had a huge set of lungs. The sound was a really low frequency to start with, then turned into a higher shrieking yell that made my hair stand up.

"What the heck?" Carl whispered.

We both sat there in silence, listening. Finally, I said, "Probably somebody camping way over there horsing around."

"Geez, I hope so," Carl replied. "Cause if it ain't, I'm wondering what in hell it could be."

A chill ran up my spine, for the first time ever. I've been in some bad situations and never had a chill run up my spine. Even though we were camped by a small stream, we could hear this thing over the burbling noises.

We just sat there, quiet, and then the howling came again, but this time, a bit closer. We both really listened up, wondering what it was.

I whispered to Carl, "Man, that sure is weird. It sounds like it's coming in closer."

He didn't answer because he was listening to the howl again. To me, it sounded like a combination of a wolf and a bull, kind of a snarling low sound, but drawn out almost into a bellow. It would go on and on for twenty or thirty seconds.

I was getting worried. Were there wolves in this country? Supposedly not, but maybe a few still existed. But for some reason that didn't seem right, as it had to be a large animal making such a loud drawn-out sound that would carry like that.

"Whatever it is, it's coming this way," Carl remarked, looking a bit nervous. He got up and poked the fire, started to put another small log on, then changed his mind.

I got up and did a camp check. My pickup keys and wallet were in my day pack, which was in my tent, and I crawled in and got them. If we had to make a quick exit, that was the one thing I couldn't leave behind. Carl saw what I was doing and did the same thing, gathering a few items and putting them into his day pack.

He then asked, "You thinking we may want to get out of here before long?"

I nodded my head yes just as the howling started again, only closer. Whatever this thing was, it wasn't shy. It acted like it wanted us to know it was coming. The howls were getting louder, and the sheer volume cut through the air like a hot knife through butter.

I sat back down, trying to figure it all out.

"Maybe it's a bull elk in rut," I whispered to Carl. "We'll feel pretty stupid about breaking camp over a bull elk."

"Whatever it is, it acts like it knows exactly where we are," Carl answered.

"Maybe," I said, "Or maybe it's just coming down the canyon for some other reason. But why would it be howling like that?"

Just then, the howling came again, but this time much closer. I could feel my heart start to beat faster. Carl jumped up, looking scared.

"Damn thing's moving fast," he said.

I got up and went back into my tent and reconsidered. If we were leaving, I wanted my nice new down sleeping bag. I quickly stuffed it into its stuff sack, then grabbed the rest of my gear—a few clothes and a warm jacket. I went back out and crammed everything into the carrier on my ATV.

Carl was shoveling dirt onto the fire. I walked over and poured what was left in a gallon water jug onto it. The howling was now very close, and the air was echoing and the sound made my ears ring.

I was ready to hit the road. Carl had now also got his gear out of his tent and stuffed it into his ATV carrier. He stood there, looking at me, then pulled his gun out. I don't know exactly what he had, as I'm not a gun person, but it was some kind of hand gun that he brought for protection from bears. He now stood there by his ATV, looking like he was ready to shoot.

The howling was now very close, and I was scared stiff. Now we could hear the sounds of tree branches breaking as if something big was crashing through the aspens and underbrush, coming at us fast.

I panicked and jumped onto my ATV and started it up, afraid for a second that it might not start, as it sputtered a little. Carl put the gun in his jacket pocket and got on his ATV and started it.

I turned and headed down the little dirt road, my ATV lights barely enough to see where I was going, Carl right behind me. He told me later that he nearly lost it more than once, as I was kicking up so much dust he had trouble seeing anything. But there was no way we were staying.

I got a good half-mile down the road before I pulled over to make sure Carl was doing OK. He pulled up beside me and said he was fine and to keep going. Just then, we heard a deep growling next to the road, and we both took off, but this time Carl was in the front and I was bringing up the rear, which I didn't like one bit.

Another half-mile, and Carl came to a screeching halt. I nearly ran into him.

"There's something really big standing right in the middle of the road up there."

I strained to see, but the dust had caught up to us and I couldn't make out anything. Whatever it was, it was incredibly fast to not only follow us, but to actually get ahead. We sat there for a minute, then Carl started again, very slow, kind of inching his way down the road.

Suddenly, from ahead, a shriek sounded out loud and clear, cutting through the air. The thing was very close. Carl stopped, pulled out his gun, and began frantically shooting.

Now, let me say that Carl's a responsible gun owner and wouldn't shoot at anything unless he knew what it was. He was panicked, but he still shot into the air, over the head of whatever was in the road. All we wanted at that point was for it to move so we could get the hell out of there.

Whatever it was must have moved, cause Carl hit the accelerator and tore out of there. I was right behind him, and I swear that when I went by the spot where he said something had been standing, I saw a pair of red glowing eyes in the trees, eyes that were in the head of something or somebody that stood a good eight feet off the ground.

Man, that shook me up. I gunned it until I was right on Carl's bumper, and I kept looking behind me, afraid I was being followed. We were now at the main forest service road and turned back the way we had come. This road wasn't as rough, so we made good time. Neither of us stopped until we came down into the little town of Marys-vale, then Carl pulled over.

His eyes had a crazed look to them. I told him we should go back to the RV campground and see if anyone was still up. We could maybe rent a cabin for the night.

He just nodded his head yes, and that's what we did. It was the middle of the night, but we managed to get a cabin, yet I don't think either of us slept much. The next day, we loaded up the ATVs, got some breakfast on the way out, and drove straight home.

So, if you're ever on the Paiute Trail over on the east side of the Tusher Mountains out of Marysvale, Utah, and you see a little dirt road winding up into a small canyon with a little stream, go on up and see if our tents are still there.

If they are, and they're not ripped to shreds, you can have them. I don't know if we were in Gorilla Gulch or not, but if so, we sure didn't enjoy our stay there, and I'm sure as hell never going back.

[6] Up the Creek

· ·

This is a story I heard while hanging out with some friends over in Utah. I invited Chris to come on a fishing expedition at no charge to help deal with his PTSD, but he said there was no way he was ever going out in the woods again. Too bad, but completely understandable. —Rusty

I'm Chris, and I used to be a mountain biker. Back in my heyday, I did some pretty good rides and was in top condition. I miss being in great shape, but now I'm afraid to go out.

But there was a time when I loved the sport, and spent every weekend on my bike. And though I did most of my riding on back dirt roads not too far from town, I would sometimes ride on pavement, especially when I wanted to do some distance and aerobic training.

Well, one weekend I decided I'd like to go ride in the La Sal Mountains in southeast Utah. Since I lived near Salt Lake City, it was about a five-hour drive for me, but I didn't mind.

I headed out on a Friday afternoon with my bike and my Toyota, and by bedtime I was in a motel in Moab, only about twenty miles from the mountains. I used to like to camp, but that's another story.

Well, heck, maybe I should tell that story, as it might give some perspective on what happened here. In a nutshell, I used to be a park ranger, and I used to work in Yellowstone. I was a law-enforcement ranger. I'm now in an administrative office in Salt Lake and never go out into the wilds.

The reason I never go out is because I have PTSD. If you know anything about it, it's very debilitating. I still have flashbacks and panic attacks. I was gradually getting better until this most recent incident happened.

Initially, I was reassigned to an office job after having to deal with a guy who'd been killed by a grizzly up by the northeast entrance of Yellowstone, and that really got to me. But now, this most recent encounter has left me a real mess.

After the grizzly attack, I developed a deep fear of the wilderness. I'm afraid of black bears, too, as they actually kill more people than grizzlies, although that's because there are lots more black bears. Seeing someone killed by a bear is really shocking, though not as much as being killed, I guess.

Anyway, back to the biking. Most mountain bikers go to Moab to ride the desert trails like Poison Spider and Klondike Bluffs, and I'd done all that, too, but this time I just felt like getting an altitude workout. It was spring and the desert heat was already starting in, so I wanted to go where it was nice and cool.

There are black bears up in the La Sals, but I figured they would still be hibernating, and I wouldn't be up in the wilds, just on the highway that flanks the mountains. Now, after what happened, I won't even go up to a place like that.

The La Sal Mountains are part of what makes the landscape of that area so unique. They're pretty big, almost 13,000 feet high, and very picturesque, as their summits usually have snow and look like they're floating over the redrock desert below. Once you get up into them, they're really pretty with small lakes and lots of aspen trees.

After a night in Moab, I got up the next morning and had a great breakfast burrito at the local diner and headed out. What's called the Loop Road starts near Moab and cuts across the mountains, coming down in a big redrock valley and then following the Colorado river back to town.

I parked my car by Ken's Lake, a reservoir south of town, then took off on the Loop Road on my bike. It was a few miles before the road started to climb, but when it did, it just took right off, switchbacking up the mountains.

It was instant gratification for views, and I could see way out into the desert rims and canyons. It was steep enough that I had to stop a few times and catch my breath before getting up to where it turns into a more gentle climb.

Well, I was soon up in the mountain mahogany and scrub oak, and I could already feel the thinner air. I stopped and had a granola bar, though the day was still young and I typically liked to go further before stopping. But I was a bit winded and feeling the effects of my sedentary office job.

While sitting there, I felt a bit weird, but I just chalked it up to my PTSD and decided I wasn't going to let it ruin my ride. But something was telling me to turn back. I wish I'd listened.

After a break I got going again. The road began cutting through the trees, and I couldn't see out. There wasn't much traffic, just a car now and then, and a few snow banks here and there chilled the air.

I was soon high above a canyon on my left, and to my right I saw a sign that said Oowah Lake. A small dirt road took off and looked like it started climbing up a narrow drainage.

On a whim (and I have no idea why), I decided to get off the pavement and go on up the road to the lake, where I knew there would be deep forest. Maybe I was subconsciously trying to overcome my PTSD. There were times I really missed the wilds.

Instead, what happened made my PTSD worse.

I turned off the pavement onto the little road and started immediately climbing. I hadn't gone far when I came to a nice little pond on the right-hand side there. At its edge stood a doe and her fawn. They just stood there and watched me as I rode by. They were so beautiful, and I realized how much I missed the wilderness.

Soon the road started getting narrower and steeper, and it became pretty much one-lane. I hoped I wouldn't meet anyone coming down, but I soon realized I wasn't going to meet a soul, as I came to a big snowbank blocking the road.

I turned around and started back down, the part I like, the fun part. As I came by the little pond, I had gained some speed, and I startled the deer, who took off. I was watching them, amazed at how fast they were, and not paying attention to the road when I hit a bump and started skidding.

I braked, but before I knew it, I'd lost my balance and the bike was sliding under me, skidding across the road, totally out of control. I slid across the road on my left side until I went clear off the edge, then about twenty feet down the side of the hill and into the thick brush, landing partially in a small stream.

The whole thing happened in a matter of seconds. One minute, I was riding along enjoying myself, and the next I had crashed, my day suddenly turning from one of enjoyment to one of disaster.

As I tumbled down the embankment, crashing into small trees and bushes, landing half in the stream, I realized I was in deep trouble. The stream was cold as heck, and I lay there in a tangled mess.

Fortunately, the water wasn't deep, and I managed to drag myself out. It was then that I realized I might be seriously injured.

I tried to do a quick assessment of what was wrong, as I felt like I was going into shock. I could see my bike tights were pretty much shredded along my left side, revealing what looked like bad road rash along my leg. I also had road rash on my left arm from the elbow to the wrist, and it was starting to burn like hell.

But that was the least of my problems. My left thumb felt like it might be broken and was starting to swell, and I couldn't move my left arm. It, too, felt like something might be broken, as there was a deep aching pain in the bone.

I lay there for awhile, down the steep embankment, half wet, and with injuries that might be severe. I had no one here to help me but myself, and I wasn't sure I could do anything. And on top of it all, I was getting cold.

My bike was crumpled in a heap below me, which meant no one would see it and know to look for me. But it didn't matter, as there wouldn't be anyone on the road anyway, as it was closed by that snowbank.

I couldn't help myself—I started moaning. I had no idea what to do. I couldn't stay out there like this, there was no way I would last through the night. I knew it was still getting cold up at this altitude.

After awhile, I tried to stand up. Surprisingly, I was able to, in spite of my left leg being injured. Later, I was told that the crash had torn up a lot of nerves, which would take years to really heal. To this day I sometimes have tingling and itching where I skidded along on my thigh.

I stood there for a bit, unsteady, feeling like I was going to faint, holding onto a small tree, thinking I had to climb back up or die.

I gradually began inching my way up the embankment back to the road, having to sit down a number of times to keep from blacking out. It was steep, and one time I accidentally bumped my arm and almost passed out from the pain. I was coming to the painful conclusion that it must be broken.

Finally, I made it up to the road, where I sat down and rested, wondering how far it was to the main road. It had to be at least a half-mile.

I was so disoriented it's amazing I didn't start walking back up the road instead of down. I did manage to find a big stick and use it as a kind of crutch, then started slowly hobbling down the road, knowing I had to get to the main highway before dark. If no one came along, which was very possible, well, I didn't know what I would do.

But I didn't get very far. I must have passed out, as I woke up right in the middle of the road, with no idea how long I'd been there. I turned over and cried out from the pain.

It finally dawned on me that I needed to make my arm more stable so I couldn't inadvertently move it, so I took the laces from my shoes and lashed a small stick to my arm. This was really hard to do, but it now meant I wouldn't be moving my arm and having the sharp pain.

Man, I was in a world of hurt, and it was now getting later and later. I could feel the chill in the air as the sun made its way lower in the sky and the shadows came out. My wet clothes were making me shiver, and I knew this was a serious problem. I might not die from a broken arm, but hypothermia could kill me.

I then suddenly realized there was something in the bushes not far from me. At first I thought it must be the deer, but then as I struggled to see better, I could tell it was much larger and darker.

My first thought was that it was a bear—that would figure, just my luck. This made the evening chill even chillier. I know that animals can tell when you're afraid, as you put out a fear pheromone, and I sure didn't want to do that. I felt a deep sense of urgency, like I absolutely had to get out of there before dark or I would die.

I managed to hobble down the road a bit more, light-headed and woozy, with my broken arm splinted at a weird angle, kind of poking out from my side. I just couldn't help myself, and every so often I would let out a moan.

I knew this was bad, as it might signal to the bear that I was injured and easy prey. And to make things worse, my PTSD was kicking in. I could see the guy killed by the grizzly in my mind's eye again—it was all coming back and I was feeling panicky and confused.

I could hear the sound of brush and tree limbs crashing right next to me, and I knew the bear wasn't leaving, which gave me the creeps. It had to be predatory, as a regular bear would just satisfy its curiosity and move along. And I had no defense at this point, except the stick I was carrying.

I had to stop, as I felt like I was going to pass out again. As I stood there, I could hear something whacking on a nearby tree, but over on the other side of the road from the bear. My first reaction was to think there was a woodpecker nearby—until the bear next to me started whacking on a tree, also, as if in reply.

Uh oh, I thought, there must be more than one of them. But then I realized that bears don't have hands, and there's no way they could pick up a stick and whack on a tree with it. There had to be people out there, and they were messing with me.

I called out, "Hellooo, anybody out there?"—but no one answered. I wanted to keep quiet and hide so no one could find me, but I was too messed up.

I had to keep going. I forced myself to continue down the road, kind of shuffling, and I could hear whatever it was continuing through the bushes alongside me.

Suddenly, something big came crashing from the forest straight for me—it was a large branch that was a good eight inches thick! The thing had thrown it at me, nearly hitting me square on, just missing me by a few inches. And I say thing, because there was no way a human could've thrown something that big that far and with that much force.

I tried to move faster, but couldn't. Next came a rock, once again barely missing me. By now the sun had nearly set and I could feel the cold air from the stream below. I felt like I was having a weird dream—nothing felt real.

I finally kept going, the fear of being attacked motivating me. But what happened next nearly paralyzed me with fear. All of a sudden, this thing stepped out of the brush about ten feet in front of me, then turned and looked straight at me. I'll never forget the look in its eyes—a mixture of curiosity and intelligence.

I had a very clear view of it, and there's no question in my mind what I saw and that it was very real. It had wide shoulders and towered over me, and was covered with dark brown hair with light gray hair around its face. It was massive.

As it stood there, all I can recall thinking is how in the heck can a creature this large find enough food to survive? Then it suddenly occurred to me that maybe I was going to be its dinner, and I started shaking uncontrollably.

After a few seconds that seemed more like hours, it turned and screamed at me, and the sound nearly knocked me down. It then ran down the embankment to the stream, still screaming.

And now I could see another in the shadows to the right of me. I could hear it crashing through the brush, and it sounded huge. Before I could even scream, it was on me, and I could feel it attacking—its giant teeth cutting through my skin like a knife, right through my broken arm and my injured leg at the same time with indescribable pain. I screamed again, then I passed out.

I awoke to someone standing over me, asking if I were OK. I was on the edge of the Loop Road, and a car sat in the darkness, idling, its lights shining into the thick forest.

How I got there I have no idea. I know I didn't walk there, as I was still on the Oowah Lake road when I passed out. Somehow it had to be the work of the creatures I was so terrified of.

A young couple helped me into their car, then drove me to the hospital in Moab. They'd been out sightseeing and were getting back late and just happened to see me there crumpled on the edge of the road.

The attack had been a hallucination, but I didn't realize it until later. About all I remember was a haze of doctors and IVs and needles and then surgery on my arm. I was later told by the nurses that I'd been talking through it all, describing being attacked by a Bigfoot. It had scared the crap out of a couple of them, though they weren't sure what to think. The other nurses thought I'd been hallucinating from the shock and hypothermia.

I was there for a week, then my girlfriend and her brother came down to pick me up. I told them about my bike, and they were determined to go get it, even though I didn't want them anywhere near those mountains. I waited at their motel while they drove back up there, as there was no way I could force myself to go.

When they got back, I noticed they didn't have my bike. Sure enough, they'd found it, but said they couldn't retrieve it, as it was twisted around a tree.

I thought about this later, in fact, I still think about it all the time, and I have nightmares a lot. But the creatures must have been trying to scare me away, and when they realized I was injured, they actually helped me by carrying me to the main road. There's no other explanation.

Thinking about that is helping me deal with my PTSD, but I still have a long ways to go.

I assume the bike's still there. If you want to go see it, just go about a half-mile up the road to Oowah Lake and look down to the stream. It's bright red, so you shouldn't miss it.

But I wouldn't stay long, if I were you.

[7] Cement Shoes

· ·

*I heard this weird story from an older guy in his 70s, who
was fishing the Missouri River up in Montana. We'd run into
him on the bank there and invited him to our campfire dinner
that evening. He was a really interesting guy, as he'd been all
over the place after he retired and had some good fishing spots to
share with us.*

*I will say I was pretty skeptical about his story, but he seemed
genuine when he told it, not like someone who would prank you,
so I'm now inclined to think it very well could be true. If so, there
may be a weak spot in that dam that no one's aware of. Look out
below! —Rusty*

The story I'm about to tell, well, I'm guessing you just won't
believe it. If I hadn't been there and seen it, I wouldn't believe it either. It's just too outrageous.

I promised to never mention it as long as my friend,
who had been the boss, was alive, and now that's he's gone,
well, it just doesn't really matter if I tell it or not, because
nobody's going to believe me, anyway.

I was one of the workers on the Glen Canyon Dam near Page, Arizona. Page is a pretty good sized town these days, a center for recreation on Lake Powell, which was formed by the dam.

The Glen Canyon Dam is a concrete arch dam, modeled after Hoover Dam, built for generating hydroelectricity and water storage. Page was the company town that was built to house and take care of the dam workers.

Some people would say "damn workers," because it was a very controversial dam back then and still is. It flooded Glen Canyon, which I never saw, but which was supposed to be really beautiful and is now under Lake Powell. I bet there's now a gazillion beer cans at the bottom of that lake.

Now let me say that, as far as I know, every major dam project in the United States has cost some lives. It's dangerous work. I don't know how many died at Glen Canyon Dam.

I've heard it was around twenty, but I do know of one death that I saw in person, and I will never be able to erase that image from my mind. I'm 73, so that's a long time for something to bother you.

I was one of the concrete workers, a somewhat dangerous grunt job, and I was just a kid, about 22. The work went on 24 hours a day until the dam was 710 feet tall, then it was done.

A lot of people think you just pour concrete in and fill up the dam, which is true, but it has to be done in many steps. That dam was built with about 3,000 blocks of concrete, each about the size of a house. This went on with many rows of blocks being built at the same time.

Huge buckets of cement would come off these cables from huge towers way up on top of the cliffs, where the cement plant sat. The buckets were remote controlled, which contributed to the danger. They would come down the cables off those big towers and automatically dump into the forms, then we would smooth it all out.

You had to watch what you were doing so not to get in the way of the buckets, which carried about 24 tons of concrete each. You'd get killed if you didn't.

It was a crazy place to work, and in retrospect, we didn't even get paid that well. But when you're 22, everything seems like it's just a stepping stone to a future of plenty of money and whatever you want. You're just not very realistic.

So, anyway, here's what happened. It was late in the evening, and almost time for the next shift to come on. Everyone was tired and looking forward to calling it a day. I was kind of leaning back, taking a little break and waiting for the next bucket of cement to arrive, when I noticed what looked like someone climbing down the cliffs above the dam. At this point, the dam was maybe halfway done, coming only part way up the steep cliffs about 400 feet.

I figured it was someone climbing to test the rocks or something like that, as there was always something going on. But as I watched, I saw a second climber coming down, and it really looked like the first one was being pursued. Both were going unreasonably fast for the conditions, as it was pretty much a sheer cliff.

The first guy was practically sliding, and I couldn't see very well at that distance, but it looked like he didn't have any rope. The cliff was way too steep to be climbing without a rope, so I wondered what was going on. And the second guy didn't look to be roped, either.

Then it dawned on me that these guys, they weren't climbing like a human would, but rather just coming down that steep high cliff like giant monkeys, using what appeared to be really long arms to swing down and reach across.

I looked around, and nobody else seemed to have noticed what was going on. I was working the form that was right at the side of the canyon, right straight under where these guys were coming down. Where I was working was now in the shadows, as the sun was setting, and the two guys were coming down the shadowy side of the cliff right above me.

As I watched, the first guy stopped and looked around, and it was like the first time he'd ever seen the dam and everything going on. He stopped and just hung there, looking down at everything. When the second one saw what he was doing, he tried to use the pause to catch up, and he swung down closer to the first one.

Well, they were now down far enough that I could start to make them out better. They looked to be about six-feet tall, and they were covered from head to toe in an off-white, which I thought was odd.

I realized how long the arms were on these two in comparison to normal arms on a human. That was when I began to think maybe I was looking at some kind of animal.

I looked around to see if anyone else was watching these guys, but nobody else seemed to notice. Just then, a bucket came in, and everyone got busy smoothing the cement. I slacked off and watched the drama on the cliffs.

Well, here comes my boss. He was a hardass, and he'd noticed I wasn't doing anything. And even though it was the end of the day, he had to be sure they got every penny's worth out of us.

When he asked me what I was doing, I just pointed to the cliffs. It took a minute for his eyes to adjust to the shadows, but he then saw what I was looking at. After he watched for a bit, he just stood there with me, saying, "I'll be damned."

By now, the two figures weren't that far above us, maybe a couple of hundred feet or so. Everyone was now picking up to leave, as the last bucket had been poured and smoothed. The two climbers had stopped and were just hanging there, one about thirty feet above the other.

The boss and I just stood there, watching the cliffs, as everyone else took off. There was a bit of a lull between shifts, so he and I were the only ones who saw what happened next.

The action started back up, with the first figure now climbing on down, the second one close on his heels. They were now directly above us, and we backed up as far as we could get to avoid them, but they were coming right down where we were at, on the edge of the dam. They had nowhere else to go.

The first figure now paused for a moment, looking like he was trying to figure out where to go. His only option was to come onto the dam. As agile as he was, I figured he shouldn't have any problems crossing the forms and just going on up the other side of the cliffs.

As he paused, the other guy went for him, lunging at him, almost dropping straight down onto him. For a minute, I thought they were both going to fall, and my first thoughts were about all the work we'd have to do to fix up the mess they were going to make.

In retrospect, I find that really funny, that I would worry about something like that, but that just shows how bully the management was, that we would put our work above everything else.

My boss was now cussing up a storm, asking me what it was we were seeing. I told him I had no idea, but we'd better stand as far back as we could, because they were going to cross the dam right where we were standing.

At the time, all the action was so engrossing that I really didn't have time to process what I was looking at and what it could be. I spent a lot of time later on that subject, and it bothered me a lot, but not until later.

Well, here they came, the one hot on the trail of the other. They swung down off the cliffs and ran right smack in front of us. I could've reached out and touched them. They were tall, maybe six and a half feet, with long dirty blonde hair that hung off their arms. I would guess they weighed about 500 pounds each, as they were real bulky, but also very muscular.

As the first one ran across in front of us, it had long powerful strides and its arms looked like someone who was power walking, swinging back and forth. I was amazed to see how quickly it went, and it didn't look at us or make any kind of eye contact. I got the feeling it was very frightened.

When the second one came by right after it, it turned and looked at my boss, and I got the feeling it was very aggressive and would've harmed us if it weren't so focused on catching the first one.

Now they were past us, and the one behind was gaining a bit. They were running across the forms just as agile as can be, which amazed me, considering their size. It sure looked like the one doing the chasing was angry, and man, I wouldn't want that guy mad at me. The boss and I just stood there in shock.

These gorilla guys were now halfway across the dam, when I noticed movement from above. Sure enough, here came a bucket of cement! The second shift should've been there by then, but they hadn't arrived yet for some reason. Since it was all automated, the bucket was right on schedule.

That bucket swung down and before I could even blink, it had barely missed the first guy and had slammed full-on into the second with a sickening thud, taking him right off the edge of the form and into the middle of the poured cement, then dumping 24 tons of cement right smack on top of him.

We were a few forms over, but I could see this creature flailing his arms, trying to get out, but sinking fast. He let out a scream that shook the dam, or so it seemed, and it echoed off the cliffs.

The first creature stopped and turned back, now aware that something had happened. I could see it pause and start to turn back when he figured out what had happened, as if he was going to help the first figure, but he then turned and continued running across the dam. He was gone and up the other side of the cliffs in record time.

In the meantime, we just stood there, wondering what to do. The creature who'd fallen into the cement was deathly quiet, and we wondered if he were still alive or not. It was too far and too dangerous to go over there for a look, so we just stood there, neither of us saying a word. There was nothing we could do, anyway.

Just about then, the second shift started arriving, and we watched as the guys responsible for that form started in, smoothing the concrete. I found out later that they were late because there had been a malfunction at the entry gate. They acted as if nothing unusual was going on, so we figured the creature was buried to where they couldn't see him. That was when we got out of there.

We both went our separate ways, but the next day, the boss took me aside and said I was to never mention this to anyone. He made me promise, saying he and I would both lose our jobs. They would think we were crazy and fire us. And after that, he sure slacked up on me, giving me easy jobs to do.

I never mentioned it again, not to anyone else or to my boss. It was as if nothing had ever happened. Funny thing is, the boss guy started buddying up to me, probably because we shared the same kind of trauma, although I think it affected him more, having that ugly thing staring right at him.

We actually became pretty good friends and stayed in touch through the years. I actually helped him get a job years later, working for a construction company owned by a friend of mine. Seeing that gorilla guy did something to him. He became much more humble and sincere.

You know, thinking about this, probably every concrete dam has rumors that someone was buried in the cement during construction, some poor worker who slipped and fell. It's kind of an urban legend that makes the rounds. But when we started working at Glen Canyon Dam, they told us this was impossible, and here's why:

Even though the forms were more than big enough for someone to be buried in, it would take a lot of buckets of wet cement to fill such a form, and those buckets didn't all arrive to be poured at once.

As soon as a bucket was dumped, we'd all be there leveling it out and it would make about one foot of fresh wet cement across the house-sized form. If you fell in, you most likely wouldn't sink any deeper than that one foot, because the stuff below it was already hardening. So, for someone to be buried in the concrete at Glen Canyon Dam was basically impossible.

But what they didn't consider was the big difference between a man that weighs maybe 200 pounds and someone or something that weighs a good 500 pounds or more. That somewhat hardened concrete is sure not gonna hold them up. It's still soupy enough for something that heavy to sink into.

And it didn't help having more buckets of wet cement poured in on top. Yeah, a pretty bad way to die, and I wish I hadn't been there for that one.

But it sure ain't in the history books about Glen Canyon Dam. They say the dam will silt up in a thousand years, though I've heard it's happening way faster than that. When it does, they may just leave it as it is, but if they ever try to dismantle it, someone's gonna have a bit of a surprise when they find that big creature's body there in the concrete.

[8] Mary O'Connor

· ·

This isn't really a story of a Bigfoot encounter, at least not a first-hand one like most of the stories I hear. But the woman, Jenny, who told this had us all fascinated by the possibility that an early pioneer had actually recorded her experiences with Bigfoot in a remote part of Colorado.

I hope Jenny can recover the lost journals and will call me. If so, I'll keep you posted. It would be fun to make it into a book, if the granddaughter didn't object. Stay tuned, and in the meantime, I'm hoping it's true. —Rusty

We've all heard of the type of guy who gets tired of civilization and heads for the hills, becoming a hermit or mountain man. But what about a woman who does this? And one who's in her fifties when she heads out? And furthermore, one who ends up making friends with a group of Bigfoot in the area?

Sounds pretty outrageous, but that's the story of Mary O'Connor, the daughter of Irish immigrants who came and settled in a valley in northwestern Colorado.

Mary's story was only recently told, and that's because her granddaughter, who had inherited Mary's journals, decided to share them with a historical society in the area. For her sake, and also for the historical society's sake, I won't mention the exact location, but I was one of the lucky ones who got to read Mary's journals before her granddaughter changed her mind and took the journals back. I don't think Mary's granddaughter had any idea what was in the journals when she donated them, and the resulting publicity was more than she wanted.

I'm a history buff, and I just happened to be visiting a friend in the town nearest Mary's homestead. When I went to the historical society out of general curiosity, they told me they had just received something I might find of interest, as I'm always wanting to know more about women pioneers.

I wasn't allowed to take the journal out of the building, so I sat and read the whole thing in one sitting, wearing the plastic gloves that they issued to keep the paper free from oils. I wish now I could've somehow made a copy, but they didn't have a copier and wouldn't let me take it out, and now it's gone.

I don't know if one were to locate the granddaughter whether or not she would ever let it be read again, but I'd sure like to go back up there and try to get a copy.

What was in the journal that was so controversial? Well, most of it was just the story of how Mary went off by herself back into a little pristine valley that could only be reached by horseback and how she made a life there. She built her own cabin and grew her own food and collected her own firewood for the long winters. That in itself was remarkable, considering how difficult that would be to do back then, but that's not what made the journal unique.

After a season or two, Mary had some uninvited company come in, and that's what makes her journal both interesting and controversial. Those who refuse to believe Bigfoot exists had a problem with Mary's story and decided she'd gone off the deep end.

As I sat in that little historical society building, which had once been the original homestead cabin where the town now sits, I had no idea what I was holding in my hands. The journal was actually several small leather-bound notebooks, and the first one or two were mostly her thoughts on the weather and the daily things that go into carving a life out of the wilderness.

That was very interesting to me, as Mary was a good writer, and there were plenty of things that made you feel like you were there with her—descriptions of the sunrises and sunsets, the full moon on the deep snows in the bitter cold, how the wolves would come around her cabin at night and sleep against the outside wall to stay warm—lots of interesting details of what life was like all alone in a vast Colorado wilderness in the early 1900s.

But imagine my surprise when I got somewhere in the second or third volume and read a line that was kind of like this (and I'm quoting from memory, paraphrasing):

"I awoke last night to something scratching on the cabin walls right above where I slept. I was at first startled, wondering what in the world it could be, but my fright soon turned to curiosity. I figured it was some sort of critter."

"I got my rifle and slowly opened the door just a crack, where, much to my surprise, I saw a giant hairy beast just standing there. For some reason, I surmised it was a male of the species, and when he turned to look at me, he seemed as surprised as I was. He was very thin and seemed to understand what a rifle was and looked frightened until I set it aside, then I saw what looked to be a plea. I went back in and got some dried ears of corn I'd been saving for my dinner and threw them out to him, whereupon he grabbed them and ran away."

Well, you can imagine the effect this had on me! I'd been reading about the usual pioneer stuff, then all of a sudden, there was a Bigfoot in the picture, though Mary never calls him that. Her description fits Bigfoot to a tee, though, and she doesn't just have one hanging around, but eventually an entire family comes to live in the wooded area down by the stream that runs through the valley.

Well, I can recall exactly what the time of day was, what I was wearing, how cool the room was, all that kind of stuff, the details you remember when you have something unforgettable happen, something that really hits you from out of the blue and shakes up your view of the world.

I had never given Bigfoot a thought until then, it was just a myth. But here I was, reading this woman's journal, someone who had no need to prove anything nor to hoax anyone, someone who probably figured her journals would never be read by anyone but herself, writing about a mythical creature as if it were real!

I gave this a lot of thought. Maybe Mary was bored and was trying to spice up her life, but why put such a thing in her journals instead of just writing a story?

The more I read, the more I believed it was true. The level of detail was just way off the chart for someone making something up. For example, one entry read (and again, quoting from memory):

"The little ones appeared to be twins, as they were both the exact same size, and I couldn't tell them apart. Of course, telling animals of another species apart is never easy unless you belong to that species, especially when they're covered with thick hair from top to toe. But what I surmised to be the little girl seemed to have a bit smaller face, and she seemed a bit more reclusive and shy than the boy, which I now take to be a general characteristic of this species."

"I've often been very happy to know that they're like this, gentle giants, especially after they decided to become my neighbors. And better neighbors I've never had. I always felt safer with the gentle beasts there, for I knew they would protect me from any harm. And though their daily begging soon wiped out my corn supply, they still were very kind to me, asking nothing in return, the little ones coming daily to bring me sweet little gifts, such as pretty rocks and flowers. I decided then and there to stock up on sugars and things of that nature when I next went into town to give as treats in return."

Mary talks about the Bigfoot family as if they were human, and if what she recounted was true, they were smart and had many of the same characteristics as we do. In some ways, they seemed better than we are—they were not violent, and the parents were very kind and loving to their twins. She doesn't mention what they ate other than her own supplies (which they quickly wiped out and she had to start rationing).

The next summer, Mary enlarged her garden and stored a lot of vegetables and such for the next winter, some for the Bigfoot. She also developed a way to communicate with them, though it was kind of rough, but it proved they could think and plan the future and had strong emotions, just like we humans do.

The communication involved tapping and knocking and head nodding and stuff like that, but it served to get the point across. For example, when Mary would ask what they wanted, they would grind two rocks together to ask for corn, as they had seen Mary grinding her corn with an old metate and mano she'd found near the cabin. They would often knock on trees with big sticks to tell her someone was coming. When they wanted Mary to know they felt bad, they would mimic Mary crying, as they'd seen her do when mourning a pet magpie she'd been feeding that died. She went into all this in the journal, and it's fascinating.

Anyway, I won't go on and on, but I sure wish I had a copy of those journals. I'm hoping to get back to Colorado this coming summer and see if I can hunt them down. If so, I'll give you a call. I suspect the descendants of that family are still living in the area, and by that, I don't mean Mary's family, but rather, the Bigfoot.

And I wouldn't mind meeting some of them, too. After what Mary wrote, I don't think there's anything to fear. It kind of makes me want to go build a little cabin way out in the woods in northwestern Colorado.

[9] All Shook Up

· ·

This was quite a story, and it scared the bejeebers out of me while the fellow, Chuck, told it. We had just enjoyed one of my great dutch-oven dinners and were having a beer over a camp-fire, not far from my home town of Steamboat Springs, Colorado.

I asked Chuck if he and his wife still camped, and he said they did and have never had anything like that happen before or since. I was glad he was as prepared as he was and I was tempted to ask him for some of his secret weapons, but didn't, as it would've been illegal. But carrying something like that could sure come in handy in the right circumstances. —Rusty

My wife and I are retired and hail from Wyoming, where my kids now run the family ranch, though we still live in the old ranch house when we're not traveling. We've worked really hard all our lives, and when the time came for us to retire, we bought a travel trailer, a real nice 26-foot Dutchman with everything we needed, including a bath-room, nice kitchen, and lots of space.

We had toyed with getting a fifth wheel, but decided on a bumper pull, since that way we wouldn't have to modify my Ford F-350 pickup by adding a hitch in the bed. That truck had put in a lot of ranch work and I knew exactly what kind of shape it was in, what needed replacing when, that sort of thing, and I also had a nice locking toolbox installed in the back. I didn't want to change anything on it, and it already had a bumper hitch, so the bumper-pull Dutchman trailer was what we ended up with.

The contents of that toolbox in the back of my ranch pickup would save the day for us later, unbeknownst to me.

We like the West, so we usually travel in Idaho and Montana in the summer and then go to Arizona for the winter. This happened in July, I believe, and we were near the town of Swan, or Swan Lake, can't recall what it's called exactly, but it's in the beautiful Swan Valley of Montana, not too far from Flathead Lake.

Swan Lake is a large lake there, some ten miles long, and it's surrounded by heavy timber. We had pulled onto a back road on the west side of the lake and found a nice little spot to camp and were going to spend a couple of days there. We weren't that close to the lake, as we worried about mosquitoes, plus it's a popular boating area and we didn't want the noise.

We were the only folks around, which is how I like it. I love remote areas because they're so peaceful. We almost never stay in parks because of the racket and people every-where, plus we just can't afford the price every night.

So, we set up camp, which mostly meant just getting out the camp chairs and kicking back. The mosquitoes weren't too bad, and our little Corgi, Jimmy, was running all over and sniffing all around the camp, having a ball. That little dog loves camping.

It was a pleasant day, but we had no idea what was in store for us that night—it was to be a night we would never forget.

My wife and I sat around after a dinner of barbecued hamburgers and potato salad, just talking and enjoying ourselves. We'd driven quite a ways that day and were tired, so we hit the hay a bit early, and it wasn't long until we were sound asleep, little Jimmy tucked down by my wife under the covers, where he always sleeps. Corgi's don't have real long hair and he always wanted to get down under where it's warm.

Well, about two in the morning, I had to get up and go pee, which is becoming more and more the case with me as I get older. But no big deal, I just quietly got up and went into the bathroom. But as I stood there, I remember thinking we had a skunk outside and it had sprayed pretty close. The smell was really strong, and in retrospect, that's probably what woke me up and the peeing was just an afterthought.

Well, no way was I going to open the door and look out to see where a skunk was, so I just pulled back the curtain a bit to see if anything was out there. It was a dark night, no moon, and I didn't see a thing, so I went back to bed, thinking we'd have to be careful with Jimmy if there were skunks around. I was soon asleep again.

I don't know how long I'd been asleep, but I woke up with Maggie, my wife, poking me in the ribs, telling me there was something outside. I told her it was a skunk, but she said it was too big to be a skunk, even though she could smell the skunk, too.

I got up again and looked out the window. Not a thing. I walked to the other side of the trailer and looked out that side. Nothing. I went back to bed, and asked Maggie what she'd heard. She said it sounded like people outside whispering.

Well, that sure set me on edge. Bears and such will take off if you scare them, but people messing around camp could be trickier. I couldn't imagine anyone being this far out in the sticks, like high-school kids pulling a prank or something. I thought about drug growers, but I hadn't heard anything bad about the area. I would suspect that the growing season is too short in Montana for much of anything like that.

As I lay there, wondering what Maggie had heard, I heard it myself. It did sound like someone whispering, just outside our bedroom window, no less, which was closed, as Montana summer nights can be a bit chilly. Maggie poked me in the ribs, and I grabbed her hand, my way of saying be quiet and don't move.

We both lay there, and now Jimmy was crawling out from under the covers. I grabbed him, as I didn't want him to start barking. I figured it would be best for whoever was out there to not know we could hear them, as it might give us a bit of edge.

I held onto Jimmy, and I could feel him shaking like a leaf. He wanted Maggie, so I kind of pushed him over to her, whispering for her to not let him bark. Jimmy was a brave little feller, and I'd seen him bark at bears, so for him to be so scared puzzled me.

Just then, the whispering started in again, and it sounded like two people talking to each other, but something was off. I could make out soft sounds, but it was like they were in a foreign language. Whoever it was, they were just outside our window, not more than a few feet from our heads.

Well, that was enough for me. Like I said, I'm an old Wyoming rancher, and I've carried a rifle all my life. It's just what you do when you have a ranch with animals that can be easily killed by predators.

So, I quietly got up and went into the living room and got my rifle out of the case I keep it in. I loaded it and then crept over to the window and peeked out, trying to see towards the back of the trailer where our bedroom was. I couldn't see a thing.

The noise had stopped, almost as if they knew we were awake. As I stood there, I realized how vulnerable we actually were. If someone wanted to mess with us, they could damage the truck, like maybe let the air out of the tires, and we would be sitting ducks. I've never worried much about camping out like that before, but people are getting crazier, so maybe it wasn't an irrational worry.

But I was still puzzled why anyone would come clear out where we were parked to mess around when there were others camped much closer to the highway and who were also camping alone, just like we were. I always figured the further out you were, the safer.

I went back into the bedroom, where Maggie was slipping out of her pajamas and into her clothes. I figured I should do the same, so I got dressed. I then whispered to her that she should be ready in case we need to leave, so she went around and quietly put a few things away. How she managed in the dark I don't know.

Well, all was quiet, and I was now wondering about getting out my spotlight and seeing what was out there, but I just couldn't get up the courage. I thought about this a lot later and talked to Maggie about it, and it was really unlike both of us to be so cowardly.

Normally, if someone was messing around, I would just get my gun and warn them that I was going to shoot and maybe even fire a couple of times into the air, then I would spotlight the place. But for some reason, we were both acting like scared rabbits and being very cautious. And even little Jimmy was now hiding down under the covers, still shaking.

Well, now we could make out something new. It sounded like a foreign language, like Chinese or Japanese, and this really got to me. It made me mad, thinking that someone was out there playing games with us. That's when I figured it was people, and I wondered why some foreigners would want to mess with us out in the middle of Montana.

I decided to open the front door and fire off a few rounds into the air and scare them off, but I never made it to the door because I was soon on the floor, rolling around, the rifle next to me.

My first thought was that we were having a really big earthquake! I'd never been in a quake, and this was exactly how I imagined it to be. The trailer was rocking back and forth, back and forth, and things were clattering around and falling to the floor.

It stopped, and now Maggie was next to me, shining her flashlight, helping me up. I grabbed my rifle and stood there in shock when it started again! This time I managed to land on the couch and hang onto the rifle, but the trailer was now twisting instead of rocking, and it felt like it would soon be twisted right off the hitch.

Maggie was terrified, and so was I. This was no earth-quake, something outside was doing this. But no human on earth had that kind of strength. It felt like they were actually picking up the trailer to twist it. It stopped again, and now a really loud screech filled the air around us, and I swear, that was scarier than the rocking and twisting.

I felt helpless, which isn't a good feeling. We needed to get out of there, and I wondered if the trailer was still even attached to the truck, or if it had been twisted off. There was no way I wanted to take the time to unhitch the trailer so we could leave in a hurry, and yet it would slow us down, trying to turn it around and get out of there. We were in a quandary, for sure. I will add that after that, I always parked so as to make a quick getaway.

I decided it was time to make a statement, even though I was scared stiff, so I slowly opened the front door enough to fire off a few rounds into the air. This was followed by another scream, and this scream sounded more angry than scared.

Well, Maggie's a smart woman, and she'd watched enough TV to inform me that we weren't dealing with people at all, but Bigfoot. I would've laughed at her except the evidence was pretty convincing. I'd always figured Big-foot was an invention of the media or of people trying to scare each other. I had absolutely no interest in it, nor did I believe for a second it might be real. But it did seem to explain what was going on.

Now something was pounding on the sides of the trail-er as if trying to get in. Maggie was frantic with fear, holding onto my arm so tight it made it ache, and I had no idea what to do. Should I start shooting at the sounds? Would that just make it madder? And whatever it was, there were more than one of them to contend with. But I had to do something.

Later, after doing some research on the internet, Maggie told me she didn't believe we would have been harmed, but at the time, it sure didn't feel that way. She said they were trying to get us out of their territory, but how in heck were we supposed to leave when they had us too scared to move? And it seemed like they were trying to damage our rig.

I was now worried they would break out the windows and get inside. Maggie, being the brave one in the family, took my floodlight from the cupboard and went to the side of the trailer they were on and shined it out the window.

Well, this confirmed what we were dealing with, because there, right up against the window, was a huge hairy head with glowing green eyes looking back at her. What I could see in the moment before it ducked was terrifying. It had a thick neck and its face was covered with dark-brown hair except around the mouth, nose, and eyes, and there the skin was a dark gray.

It didn't like the light and ducked down and disappeared. Maggie and I both were frozen in disbelief. She recovered before I did and started praying out loud.

I was now remembering something in my truckbox that might come in handy, if only I could get to it. I had to go outside and unlock the box in the bed of the truck, and I needed to do it quickly and without these giants knowing about it. There had to be a way Maggie could distract them.

I told Maggie about my plan, and she said there was no way to distract them, but since they seemed to hate the light, maybe she could stand there and cover me with the spotlight and they would stay back. It was risky and probably the scariest thing I've ever done, well, not probably, but for sure.

OK, we didn't forget little Jimmy in all this. We went and got his little carrier and got him out from under the covers. He wouldn't come out for me, and Maggie had to actually drag him out. We put him in the carrier, then I got my jacket on and took my truck keys and removed the key to the truckbox. I unlocked the truck doors with the remote key. After I found the lighter I used to start campfires, we were ready to rumble.

They were back, and the trailer was starting to rock again. We had to act fast. I gave Maggie my truck keys and opened the trailer door and ran to the truck, opening the door and shoving little Jimmy in. Maggie stood at the trailer door with my gun and the spotlight, covering me, but she could barely stand up, the trailer was rocking so hard.

Now she ran and got into the truck with Jimmy, starting it, while I tried to unlock the truckbox. The trailer was causing the truck to rock with it, and I had trouble getting the box open. But just as I opened it, the rocking stopped. They were on to us.

I now saw a huge figure coming up towards me from the back of the trailer, and I froze in fear. But Maggie shined the light back and just sat on the horn at the same time. The figure stopped just long enough for me to grab what I needed from the box and jump into the passenger side. Maggie was pulling out just as a huge bulky figure ran around and stood in front of us, blocking our way.

Maggie put the truck in reverse, backing the trailer around so we could leave. I was in shock, seeing this huge creature, but she just kicked into survival mode and kept on going. My brain finally kicked in when I saw a second figure coming up behind the trailer, and that's when I pulled out the lighter and lit the fuse.

I don't know if you're familiar with M80s, but they're like a huge firecracker. They are also illegal. They make a helluva boom, but they're also dangerous to mess with. They look a lot like a shotgun shell, but are bigger, and have a stiff fuse coming out of the middle.

I had a license from the State of Wyoming to carry them, as the wildlife department issues them to ranchers who are having their haystacks eaten by deer and elk, and we use M80s to scare them off. I kept them in my truckbox and had forgotten to take them out for the trip.

You're supposed to light them on the ground, never while holding them, but this was an unusual circumstance. I held an M80 in one hand, lit the fuse with the lighter, then threw it out the window.

Kaboom! Man, those things are loud. It felt like my eardrums were history, and the sound echoed through the forest. Maggie now had the truck and trailer turned around, and there was no sign of anything unusual around at all, no Bigfoot.

Kaboom! I threw another out the window, this time trying to get a better distance with it. Maggie was really flooring it, and the trailer was now bouncing down the road behind us. I knew our trailer leveling jacks were history, as you just can't drive off with them down, and I knew they'd been ripped from underneath the trailer. But I didn't care.

After a bit, Maggie slowed down so not to beat everything to heck. The Bigfoot were long gone. We'd probably scared them out of their skin, just like they'd done us.

When we finally got to the highway, I noticed a sheriff's deputy coming up the road with his lights flashing. It was 3:30 a.m. We pulled out onto the highway, and he stopped us. He asked if we'd heard any gunshots from down in the area we'd been in. Apparently some other campers had heard it and called it in.

I wasn't sure what to say, as I knew he would think we were crazy if we told him the truth, plus you're not supposed to be hunting or shooting after sundown and I sure didn't want to get arrested. And yet I wanted people to know what had happened in case they were in danger.

As I sat there at a loss for words, my sweet wife, who has rescued me in many a difficult situation, simply told him that we'd been next to the folks who were doing the shooting, and they'd seen a grizzly and had already left. She told him that he should warn people not to go back in there, at least not for awhile.

He thanked her, and we drove off into the night and didn't stop until we got to Kalispell, where we spent the next morning getting our trailer checked at an RV place. The leveling jacks were ruined, but we could get them fixed later. We then headed on home, now firm believers in the enigma called Bigfoot.

[10] On the Boardwalk

· ·

I must say I don't get a lot of disabled people on my flyfishing trips, for obvious reasons. And I hope I'm not being politically incorrect by calling them disabled, as there may be a better way to refer to them.

Abbie didn't seem disabled to me at all. She did things in her wheelchair that amazed me, like navigating the edge of a stream and pulling in a big trout she'd caught all by herself.

When Abbie first contacted me and wanted to learn how to flyfish, I was a bit hesitant, but afterwards, I felt inspired. She made me realize how little I really accomplish in comparison, given that I'm healthy and hale.

She told this story around a campfire, once again near my hometown in northwest Colorado. I hope Abbie comes fishing with us again, as she was a very special person and everyone loved her humility and sensitive personality. And her story was pretty special, too. —Rusty

My name is Abbie, and I can't walk, but I get around pretty well in my sport wheelchair and my modified van. There was a time when I was younger that I felt sorry for myself, but if I were able to walk, I wouldn't have had the unique glimpse of another world that I had—a world few have ever seen.

I was born with a birth defect of the spinal cord. For a lot of my early life, I lived in a very sheltered space, both mentally and physically. My parents took good care of me, but they worried about me more than they should have and overly sheltered me. If they could see me now, they would be either very proud or would die of worry.

My parents died when I was in my teens, and I ended up in a residential school for the disabled called Alpine School, which was near a ski area in Utah. My whole life turned around at that point, as I'm sure you can imagine.

When I went to live at the school, I was no longer treated like an invalid, and I was expected to do things and take care of myself. It was a really hard time for me, but it also made me grow as a person. I saw myself blossom into a new life like a butterfly.

Part of my new life included doing things outside, which was a first for me. My parents would take me for car rides or let me sit out on the patio, but actually doing anything that involved physical activity was never even considered. Oh sure, once in awhile we would go for a walk, but then only down the sidewalk near the house, with my dad pushing my wheelchair. My parents loved me, but they didn't understand what I could really do.

And when I met Aaron, my life changed even more. He was new to the school, and he was turning the place upside down, but in a good way. Aaron was 15 and his parents had brought him to live with us for awhile because they weren't sure what to do with him and feared for his safety, and maybe rightly so. He was only there for a few months, then he went back home, but in that short time he had a profound effect on me.

Aaron wanted to be an athlete, which is pretty difficult for someone who's stuck in a wheelchair. People who can walk take things for granted that are huge for someone in a wheelchair.

Aaron was a skateboarder who had recently permanently injured himself and was now a paraplegic, like me, with no use of his legs. This was really hard on him, and he vowed to not let it slow him down. And man, he didn't.

The school we were in encouraged us to live to our best ability, but they hadn't reckoned with someone like Aaron. First, he would sneak out and go down to the nearest park and hang out. Aaron missed his buddies and being in his old school. And that was just the start of the things he would do.

Aaron wanted to be back on his skateboard, and he couldn't, so he just started using his wheelchair like a skateboard, riding up and down the skateboard park in it. He ended up becoming a local hero and could do all kinds of tricks in that wheelchair. He finally got a custom-made wheelchair and ended up going home and back to his regular school and then on to college.

So, Aaron wasn't around very long, but he really inspired me. The more I got to do things outdoors, the more I loved nature and wanted to be outdoors. I decided I wanted to be a landscape and wildlife photographer, and I know that sounds hard for someone in a wheelchair, but that's exactly what I ended up doing. That's how I make my living today, and people don't know I'm disabled when they see my photos.

All of this is relevant to my story, so bear with me. The more I was around Aaron, the more I saw what I could do, and I, too, started sneaking off, but instead of going to the park, I would go over to the nearby waterfowl refuge. I was supposed to be in a class in the art building, but I told my teacher I'd dropped it, and the people who were in charge of my whereabouts all thought I was over doing art, so nobody noticed I was gone.

I would wheel over across the back grounds to the art building, then veer off down a dirt trail that connected with a beautiful boardwalk that traversed the wildlife sanctuary, which was next to our school. The sanctuary was a beautiful place, and I just loved going over there and sitting and watching the birds.

The boardwalk wound around through the refuge with places where you could stop and rest on a bench or even hide in a blind to watch the birds. It was on the edge of a large wetlands, and there were places the boardwalk went right over the shallow water. If you set there really quietly, sometimes ducks would float right up next to you. It was so cool, and I loved that place, but I never got to stay very long at a time. I never saw anyone over there.

Well, every evening, I could hear the ducks and geese making a racket before they settled in for the night, and I knew the sunsets over there would be fabulous, much better than out my window, where everything was blocked by nearby buildings. I really wanted to go over there in the evening and see what the refuge looked like.

One evening, after dinner, I was just sitting there, when Aaron came rolling by. This was only a few days before they sent him back home, saying he didn't need to be there anymore. We started talking, and I told him what I wanted to do, and he said we should just go do it. So the two of us ended up sneaking over to the refuge and hanging out until it was almost dark. We had a great time, and nobody even missed us. Aaron was really an inspiration, nothing stopped him.

A few days later, the itch to go over there hit me again. It was such a perfect place, so quiet, and so far away from all my problems. When I was over there, I forgot my life was different and that I couldn't walk. The outdoors does that to me, makes me feel whole.

So I snuck off again. Seems like after dinner and before bedtime was a good time, as nobody really checked up on me. I was soon over at the boardwalk, watching the sunset and listening to all the birds. I had a little flashlight with me, so I wasn't worried about getting home.

But all of a sudden, it got totally still. All sound ceased, no frogs, no birds, no crickets, nothing. This was a first for me, and I wondered why. What would cause everyone to be quiet all of a sudden?

Remember that I had hardly even been outdoors when this happened, so I didn't realize how totally unusual it was. I just figured that at a certain time of day, everyone got quiet. It didn't seem ominous or anything to me.

I sat there for awhile, then decided it was getting dark enough I should probably head back while I could still see and before I was missed. Just as I turned to go, I noticed a movement in the thick brush over to my left, kind of where the shoreline was. It didn't look like a bird, and I was kind of startled, as it hadn't even occurred to me that there might be other creatures in there.

I stopped and looked really hard, but couldn't make anything out, so I kept going. But as I got further down the boardwalk back towards the school, I could now hear something following along behind me. It made the boardwalk shake a little, and I could hear its footsteps, though they were muffled by the wood, but it was like something that was barefoot.

I turned around, but couldn't see anything, so I continued on. I was soon on the little dirt path and back over to the school. I ran into Aaron in the hall, and he stopped and told me he was leaving, so I forgot all about what had happened, as I hated to see him go. I later thought about it and decided there were deer over there.

Well, it was a few more days before I went back. I had now acquired a small camera from Aaron, who gave me his little pocket singleshot as a gift when he left, and I was anxious to go see if I could get some sunset photos. It was the start of my photography career, though I didn't know that.

I can't tell you how excited I was! I had just turned 16, I had a camera for the first time, and I was discovering my freedom. I rolled out right after dinner and straight for the refuge to shoot the sunset. I remember checking out the clouds all day to see if it would be a good sunset display and thinking it would.

I don't even remember if I got any pictures or not, as things changed so quickly, and I forgot all about the sunset.

It was a bit later than usual, as we'd had dinner late for some reason. I do remember that, and I was very aware of how the shadows were getting long, as I wondered if they'd make interesting pictures. But I don't recall much after that, other than sitting there in my wheelchair next to a bird blind by the boardwalk and being very very scared.

I took some photos, then wheeled on down the board-walk a ways to a bird blind, hoping to see some evening birds. But as I sat there, I could hear that something really large was coming up the boardwalk directly towards me.

I knew it was large because I could make out its shad-ow, even though I couldn't actually see it because the blind was blocking my view. I assumed it couldn't see me, and I was desperately trying to figure out how to either hide or run away, both which were impossible.

I then realized that this was the same thing I had heard previously and mistaken for deer. I also remember noting how deathly still it was all around me, just like the previous time. And I will admit the thought ran through my mind that I had been very foolish to think I could lead a some-what normal life like other kids my age. All these thoughts went through my mind as I sat there, terrified.

It was dusk, and as I sat there, this huge thing walked right up to the blind I was behind. Did it know I was there? It had to. What was it? I had no idea. I didn't know enough about the local wildlife to even guess, but I knew it wasn't human.

Now it began to make a snuffling noise, like it could smell me but wasn't sure what to think. Next, I heard a high sort of chatter, then a low growling sound, all which lasted only seconds. It was like someone was talking. There must be two of them!

I felt more and more frightened, if possible, but when a huge dark hairy head slowly looked around the edge of the blind, I almost fainted. There was nothing I could do but sit there. I wish now I'd taken some photos, but I was too scared during all this to even remember I had a camera.

Now this thing stepped around to where it was in full view, and it had a young one with it!

I remember well what it looked like. It was massive and had dark longish hair that appeared to be very well-groomed, not at all matted or dirty. It had a musky smell, kind of like a wet dog, but more swampy smelling. Its arms were very long and its eyes were very intelligent. My over all impression was that it was more ape-like than animal-like, if that makes sense. It had skin showing around its eyes and cheeks and mouth, and the skin was gray, even though the hair was a dark brown. It had a broad forehead.

The baby was just like it, only with shorter hair and of course, much smaller. It was cute in an ugly way, or you could also say, ugly in a cute way. It clung to its momma's leg—at least I assume it was the momma and not the dad.

They both stood there, looking at me, and I began to understand how zoo animals must feel, being stared at by another species, captive and unable to get away. They weren't more than five feet away from me, almost close enough they could reach out and touch me.

And that's exactly what they did! The big one, who I later decided must be the mom, slowly reached her hand over towards me. I thought, OK, here we go, this is the end, and I just sat very still. But she reached out and touched the wheels of my wheelchair, then quickly jerked her hand back. When I didn't do anything, she reached out again and touched the spokes, then the tires. It was as if she was trying to figure out what it was.

I started to relax a bit, though still terrified, as I began to think maybe whatever these things were, they were just curious—and very brave, to come up to a human and reach out like that. I later decided they somehow knew I wasn't a threat, that I wasn't like other humans.

Now the little one reached out and touched my wheel, then my leg. I'll never forget the look on its face—it must have realized I was something alive from the feel of my leg. It jumped and hid behind its mom. It was actually kind of cute, though at the time I was too scared to appreciate that.

I felt less fear, so I said something like, "I won't eat you if you won't eat me," something dumb like that, as if they could understand me and as if I could harm them if I wanted to.

This made the little one stay behind the mom, and the mom backed slowly away, then turned, picked up the youngster, and walked back down the boardwalk. It reminded me of some wild animal that has never seen a human, how they might act. Cautious but curious.

This all happened much faster than I can even tell it. And there I sat, alone again. It was nearly dark, so I got out of there and back as fast as I possibly could.

I wanted so badly to talk to Aaron, but he was gone, and there was no one else around to talk to. What were these things? Where did they come from? Would they harm me if I went back? Was I stupid enough to go back?

I slept very little that night. Now, given the internet, I would've known right away they were Bigfoot, but this was before one could just turn on their computer and research such things.

The next day, I couldn't eat, and I felt very anxious. I kept thinking I was going insane and hadn't seen anything at all, just imagined it. I wanted to go back, but I was too scared. I felt like a tornado had mixed up my brain, and nothing felt the same.

I stayed in that night with the curtains on my window closed and listened to music, trying to regain some normalcy. But I couldn't sleep again, and I was a wreck.

It was about two or three in the morning when I got up, pulled myself into my wheelchair, and started down the hall. I had to go back and see if these things were real or if I was going nuts. That shows you the state of mind I was in, to want to go back over there in the middle of the night, but I was feeling desperate. It was probably a good thing, but all the doors were locked. I finally got back into my bed and went to sleep for a few hours.

The next day, I hatched up a plan. If I had really seen these creatures, they seemed like they weren't interested in harming me, so why not see if I could make friends with them? I snuck into the kitchen and stole a bag of apples, hiding it under my shirttail, then taking it back into my room.

After dinner, I was off. I went straight to the blind where I'd seen them before and waited until it was dusk.

When everything suddenly went quiet, I knew they were back, which terrified me and made me wonder why I was so stupid as to be back over there again.

I couldn't see nor hear them, but I knew they were there. I opened the bag of apples and slowly dropped them, one by one, into a small pile, then rolled back a ways and waited. It wasn't long until they were back, the mom and her little one, who was riding on her big hip.

The mom stooped down and picked up an apple and took a bite, then ate it in one chomp. She then gave one to the little one, who ate it in two bites. They devoured that small bag of apples in just a couple of minutes.

I wasn't brave enough to stick around, so I took off as fast as I could, every once in awhile looking over my shoulder to see if I was being followed.

I was soon back to the school, only to discover I'd been locked out. Someone had done the lockdown early! Oh man, I was up the creek. My freedom was probably about to end.

I had two choices: spend the night outside and hope nobody missed me, or yell for help and bang on the door. I suddenly thought of Aaron. What would he do? No way he would risk losing his freedom. I decided to stay outside all night. It was summer and I sure wouldn't freeze or anything.

I rolled my chair over onto the patio where I couldn't be seen, then sat there, thinking about everything. I knew it would be a long uncomfortable night sitting in that chair, but I didn't care. I had actually never spent one night of my life outside, and I was curious as to what it would be like.

As I sat there, the night sky opened up, and I saw the stars in all their beauty for the first time in my life. I had no idea they were even there, not like that, anyway, layer after layer of jewels hanging there. It was incredible.

I thought of the creatures I'd seen over in the refuge and wondered what they were and what their lives were like. I decided I would continue to take them food when I could.

The next thing I knew, it was dawn, and I'd slept like a baby with my head kind of leaning against the chair back, not too uncomfortable. I had never seen the sunrise, and there it was, a real fireball. I felt like my life had just begun with all these new miracles.

As I sat there, waiting for someone to unlock the door so I could sneak back in, I heard a call from the refuge, and somehow I felt it was just for me. It was a long drawn-out whooping that would have scared me to death normally, but instead, it seemed like a good morning call. It was really different, though, as it sounded like it was made of two tones at once, a high and a low one. I wanted to whoop back, but I knew someone would hear me inside and I'd be caught.

In retrospect, it must have been a farewell whoop, as I never saw the pair again, even though I went over there a number of times. I did finally get caught and had my freedom curtailed, but it wasn't long after before I graduated from Alpine School and was accepted into a photography school, where I could follow my dreams. I even got a scholarship.

I've often wondered if somewhere out there, deep in the wild forests, a Bigfoot sometimes thinks of her childhood and wonders if it was all a dream or if her mom actually did take her right up to a human once, where she reached out and touched it.

[11] Let them Eat Steak

This story was told over a great campfire along the banks of the Roaring Fork River in Colorado, true blue-ribbon fishing if there ever was any.

The storyteller was a retired trucker named Joe who was quite the character. I asked him if this incident had made him quit trucking, and he said no, that he drove that pass many more times in his career and never saw a thing, but he sure never did stop there again. —Rusty

Since I was a little kid, I wanted to be a truck driver. I have no idea why, as nobody in my family drove truck. My dad was a mechanic, and my mom was a teacher. She always wanted me to go to college and make something of myself, but all I wanted to do was drive truck.

I think maybe it was my Uncle Jim's doing, as he was always playing these rockabilly honky tonk songs about truck drivers, songs like "Truck Drivin' Man." I hung out a lot with him in his garage, as he liked to restore old cars, and I enjoyed helping.

But to tell you the truth, I've always been very solitary, and in another era, I probably would have been like Thoreau and headed for the hills, or in his case, the pond.

So truck driving had that appeal, in that I could make a living and not have to be in an office or deal with people much. And I've always had a bit of wanderlust. I remember standing on the hill behind our house and longing to see what was over the distant mountains. The fact that my family never went anywhere probably helped the cause.

So, I went straight from high school into truck driving, and after I got some experience and my CDL license, I bought my own semi cab, on credit, of course, with my Uncle Jim cosigning. My dad wouldn't do it, because he said Mom would be mad.

I was all of 22 years old when I started driving a big Mack cab with a sleeper. I'd hit the big time, and I loved it. I was also massively in debt, but I paid it all off within about five years and was then the proud owner of my own rig. I now had my Class A CDL and medical card, insurance, and belonged to the TVC motorclub (they fight tickets on your behalf).

Initially, I drove for a nationwide trucking company, which if I were to mention the name, you would say, oh yeah, seen them all over. But then I went to work for a small company that would hire me by the job, and I seemed to make more money at this, as they didn't skim as much off the top.

I also had a more erratic schedule, which I liked, as I didn't mind working a lot and then having some time off. The other guys all had families and mortgages to pay, but I liked going fishing once in awhile. So, I would go on these long hauls, work my tail off and drink lots of coffee, then go fishing for a few days.

Well, one day I got the call to truck some meat from a meat-packing plant in Denver over to Salt Lake City. The company that regularly handled this route was having some truck problems, and this was a one-time backup deal.

So, I headed to Cheyenne from my home base, where I picked up a big Great Dane reefer, which is what you call a refrigerated trailer.

The reefer was loaded up with lots of beef steaks and such, ready for somebody's barbecue, as it was about July when this happened. The time of year contributed to the story, as you'll see, because it was hot. Driving a reefer meant you had a tight schedule to keep, as fresh produce and meats have to get to market pretty fast, so the company needed me over there right away.

Well, after I got to Denver and the reefer was loaded, I headed out on I-70, which runs straight across Colorado into Utah. It wasn't going to be a long run, but it would be an overnighter. I would just pull over somewhere and use my sleeper, then get into Salt Lake the next day.

I had started out really early, so it was early afternoon by the time I left Denver. I Made it to the Utah state line in good time, and was in Green River by dark, where I stopped at the Westwinds Truck Stop for dinner. They have good trucker-type food, and I've spent many a night in their big parking lot, especially in the winter when waiting for the roads to be cleared.

When I'm hauling reefers, I always check the gensets when I stop for gas or food, as you sure don't want any problems that way. In case you don't know, gensets are the diesel-powered generators that run the cooling systems on the truck trailers, keeping everything from getting warm. And on that hot July day, having those gensets fail would've been an expensive disaster, with all that meat in there. And that's exactly what happened, as you'll see.

So, after dinner I checked that the gensets were running OK, then got back on I-70. Before long, I turned off the freeway onto State Highway 191, which goes on up to Salt Lake City. I figured I wouldn't make it all the way and I'd have to stop for the night, but I preferred to get as far as I could so the next day wouldn't be too long, as I wanted to unload and get back home.

It's not a bad road, at least not in the summer, and I was soon rolling on through the town of Price and heading up Soldier Summit, the pass over the Wasatch Mountains. By the time I got to the pass, I was within just a few hours of my destination.

I always like that stretch of road across Soldier Summit, as the railroad pretty much follows the highway, and I like watching the trains. So, I got to the top of Soldier Summit and decided that was it for the day. I pulled over into a big wide area, checked the gensets, then crawled into my sleeper, pretty tired.

Like I said, the gensets appeared to be working, but the compressor on the refrigeration unit had quit, so all that meat had been basically getting warmer and warmer all day while I thought everything was fine.

That was the cause of all my problems, that darn compressor quitting, because that meat was starting to get a bit rank and attracted a certain kind of wildlife I never even knew existed. But I crawled into that sleeper, thinking everything was just dandy and went right to sleep.

I woke up around three a.m., which I never do. I usually sleep all night like a baby. But something had woke me up. When you're sleeping out by the highway, you tend to be a little more aware than when you're in a truck stop lined up with a bunch of other trucks.

I had no idea why I was awake. I was still tired, and I soon fell back asleep. But not for long, as it felt like the truck was moving. Man, that will get your attention! I was out that bunk like a bat out of hell, but when I looked out the window, all was fine. The truck wasn't moving at all. I decided I must've been dreaming, so I crawled back into bed.

But now I was wide awake. The adrenaline of thinking the truck was rolling had given me a buzz, and I couldn't go back to sleep. At least that's what I thought it was, but in retrospect, it was my instincts telling me something was wrong.

As I lay there, I felt it again. I wasn't dreaming, the truck had moved! It felt like something very big had stepped on the rear causing the cab to lift up just a tad, and it had definitely moved.

OK, this was really weird, because there's nothing that could cause a big loaded reefer to move like that. At first, the thought of UFOs crossed my mind, because I was way out in the middle of nowhere, sitting on the top of that pass, and there was no traffic that time of night, so it had to be aliens.

Man, that shook me up, thinking like that. I'll tell you why—because I didn't believe in aliens! To think I was being messed with by something I didn't believe in was kind of unsettling. Stories of people being abducted started to cross my mind, and I didn't want to go there.

I got up and got dressed. If I were going to be abducted, I sure wasn't going to be dropped off later in the middle of some field wearing nothing but my t-shirt and shorts. Thinking about this later makes me laugh. It's funny what goes through your mind when you're scared to death.

I sat there in my sleeper, listening for weird sounds, you know, like anti-gravity UFO engine sounds. That's what I expected to hear—maybe a loud whining sound above me or something like that. Of course, I couldn't hear anything through the constant low rumble of the gensets.

But then all of a sudden I could hear something, and that was because it was really loud and drowned out the gensets. It was the sound of metal being torn, there's no other way to describe it. It was a wrenching ripping shearing of metal sound, and while it was going on, the truck again felt like something was jumping up and down in the rear, causing the cab to come up just a bit.

I had to do something! It now sounded like my truck was being ripped apart! Now that I was more awake, I became more logical, and the thought that I was being hijacked entered my mind. Someone was breaking into the reefer and stealing the meat!

I was now more worried than when I thought it was a UFO. Aliens might mess with you, but they probably wouldn't kill you. I carefully opened the sleeper door and crawled into the cab, keys in hand. I had to get out of there ASAP!

As I slid into the driver's seat, I felt the truck rise again, and now the sound of the gensets had stopped! I could now hear perfectly, and it sounded like people talking back there, though I couldn't make out the words. They sounded like nonsense, like a record being played backwards.

Now I knew I was being hijacked. I double-checked that the cab doors were locked and started the truck. If it had been a hot night, I would've left it idling to run the AC, but since my company had just started anti-idling incentives to save gas and it was nice and cool up at that altitude, the truck was off. But I was sure wishing I'd left it running.

I jammed it into gear and took off. I had no idea who was in the reefer, but they'd just have to jump, as I wasn't going to wait around.

I could now hear that I was dragging something, and it sounded like the reefer doors or ramp or something dragging along the pavement as I drove along. But no way I was going to stop, and yeah, I was getting pretty steamed at that point.

But as I started down the highway, I noticed someone was running up next to the truck. This surprised me, as by then, I was going about 30, and nobody can run that fast.

But when they got right up next to me and jumped up on my running board, I could see it wasn't no human I was dealing with!

My god, I was about two feet from the ugliest thing I've ever seen! He had a huge face, and it was all covered in dark hair, except for light brown skin around his eyes, nose, and mouth.

That's all I could see, was his face, because it was so big it took up the whole window. And he was standing on my running board, hanging onto my big rearview mirror—and screaming so loud it felt like the window was going to shatter. It hurt my ears, even though I had the cab all closed up.

I jerked my eyes away from him just long enough to see I was going over the edge. I tried to correct the truck, but it was too late. I felt really sick as I saw what was coming. The truck was going right off the highway and into the ditch, which was a good fifteen feet below.

This is it, the end, was all I recall thinking as that massive truck smashed down the bank and rolled. The thing on my running board jumped before I went over.

I have no idea what time of night it was, but thank God there was someone coming along that road, a couple going back to Salt Lake. Before I knew it, the guy was next to me, pulling me from the cab. I wasn't seriously injured, just bruised, and I managed to crawl up that embankment and back onto the road before my truck caught on fire.

I just sat there, in shock, watching my cab burn. The man and his wife tried to figure out if I were injured, and they called the State Patrol. An hour later, I was riding with them down to Price, where I got a motel and my wife picked me up the next day.

The patrolman had called the Price fire department, and the fire was soon quickly out, but my truck was pretty much totaled. The couple told the patrolman they'd seen something huge riding on my cab and trying to get in.

When he figured out I wasn't injured, he had me do an alcohol test, which I passed. On the accident report, he put that a bear had caused me to wreck. I bet that was a first!

After an investigation, what was left of the truck was hauled away. My insurance company was great, and I soon had another cab. The company I was hauling for was also insured, so that worked out OK. The reefer had been damaged beyond repair, but hadn't burned.

The really strange thing was, after it was all over, I talked to the tow truck driver, and he wondered what I'd been hauling. When I told him meat, he seemed perplexed and wondered what had happened to it all, as he said the reefer was completely empty when he hauled it off the next day.

I think I know what happened, and I think some Bigfoot clan had a real nice barbecue.

[12] The Monkey Wrenchers

This story was told by a guy who I met in the local grocery store, of all places. He saw me buying some Jack Links jerky and made a joke about Sasquatch, and one thing led to another. We were soon having a conversation out in the parking lot, and that ended up continuing over a beer in the nearby brewpub.

His name was Stan, and we both laughed about how we became friends because of our mutual interest in Bigfoot. He's now been on several of my fishing trips, and when he tells this story, things always get real quiet. —Rusty

My great-grandpa was a railroad man during a very interesting era, when the first rails were being laid across the West. But he didn't work long on the railroads, and this story will explain why.

He told this story to my dad, who in turn told it to me when I was a kid. I never thought much about it until recently, when I started hearing tales of Bigfoot existing in places besides the Pacific Northwest and Canada. I never thought there could be Bigfoot in Utah, but now I've begun to take his story a little more seriously.

My great-grandpa, Will, went to work for the Denver and Rio Grande Railroad in 1882 as a tracklayer, making the handsome sum of $2.25/day, which included room and board.

Board consisted of whatever supplies they happened to have on hand, which seldom varied and were never very palatable, and room consisted of a tent that was shared with as many men as they could pack into them. You had to provide your own bedroll. He said a lot of the guys would only use the tent if it were raining and otherwise slept outside on the ground or even made dugouts in the sides of the nearby hills or stone shelters.

I would suspect that a lot of the guys working on the railroad construction were Chinese, as this was the norm back then. A lot of Chinese labor was used, and there was always a segregation between the Chinese and the non-Chinese, as far as living quarters went. That era saw a lot of prejudices.

The railroad was laying track from the little desert town of Green River, Utah on over to an even littler town called Cleveland. Cleveland is close to the coal mines in central Utah, and the track would serve to open that area to coal traffic for the Denver and Rio Grande.

This was the era of railroad expansion, and there was a lot of competition between the Denver and Rio Grande and the Union Pacific and also the Utah Railroad. They were all fighting for the same turf, and some of that fighting had taken the form of pulling up rails and damaging each other's property, so the guys initially thought this was what was going on.

···120···

But I'm getting ahead of myself here. Green River, the nearest town to where they were working, sits on the banks of its namesake river, but otherwise is right smack in the middle of a big desert. And once you head west about twenty miles, you come to the San Rafael Reef, an almost impenetrable barrier in the form of a big sandstone wall.

That area is called the Ghost City or the Silent City by the locals because of all the huge sandstone cliffs and knobs and points. It's about as rugged as it gets, and up on top of that is a high plateau with trees and deer. This is where I think the Bigfoot they saw came down from.

At that time, there were no roads through there, just one trail going through Black Dragon Canyon, so it was pretty much like it had been since forever.

In order to avoid this big sandstone barrier, the railroad had taken a turn and was going through the northern end of the Reef, and from there they would go through Cottonwood Canyon, crossing the San Rafael River on the way.

This was a spur off the main line, which avoided the Reef entirely by heading straight north out of Green River and going on up to Price. Interestingly enough, this spur was narrow gauge. It was meant to connect directly with the coal mines.

Anyway, my great-grandpa Will and his crew were building the rail line through some pretty rugged country, but they hadn't yet got to Cottonwood Canyon, the big canyon they would have to negotiate. And they never would get there, neither.

It all started out when they got the line over the first big hills, sort of where the Reef tapered out. They had laid rail through the flat desert, which was pretty easy going, comparatively. They then had to cut grade and move rocks in order to continue on, and things really slowed down. It was hard grueling work, day after day, and the going was slow.

Well, imagine their surprise to go back out to the rails one fine morning and find their work had been destroyed! The track lay everywhere, as if it had been ripped up and flung wherever. Whoever did it, it had to be a good-sized team of guys to do that much destruction during the night.

Everyone was disturbed and puzzled. There was no transportation back in there except by horseback or foot, and they found no indication of either. They expected to find a lot of nearby tracks in the soft dirt, but found nothing. And not only was the track thrown around, but some of it had been twisted. This would be impossible for a human to do, or even a number of humans. It was a mystery, and they were befuddled.

Well, after a lot of discussion wherein the boss was just as puzzled as everyone else, they decided it had to be one of the competing railroads, though they had no idea how they did it. The boss decided they would stand guard from then on.

So, everyone carried on with their work, re-laying the rails, and that night two men stood guard, armed and hidden behind some nearby rocks. About two a.m., shots rang out, and the guards were soon running back into the camp, excited and scared.

They had heard talking, and they then fired shots, but they knew they were outnumbered from the way the sounds came from all around them, so they hightailed it.

And to make things more interesting, the talk was in Chinese.

Oh man, that shook things up. First off came a quick roll call to make sure all the Chinese workers were there, which they were. Next came talk about the competing railroads having hired Chinese workers to tear up the rails, which didn't set well with the Chinese workers in camp, nor did it help the ongoing prejudices any.

An armed posse of sorts was quickly formed and headed back out to the rails, which were a half mile or so away. By the time they got there, the very same rail they had just laid that previous day had been torn up and twisted, and it hadn't taken all that long to accomplish, as it hadn't been long since the guards had fired the shots.

There was again no sign of anyone, and the next day revealed nothing, even when they branched out a bit and looked around the hills. No footprints. It was eerie.

Everyone worked extra hard that day, as they were now getting seriously behind schedule. That next night, they set out four guards, two to go back and alarm the camp and two to stay and shoot. One of the guys was Chinese, included so he could interpret the talking. My great-grandpa Will happened to be one of the four.

But something different happened that night. As the four guys sat there, each in a different spot, they could hear a howling sound coming closer and closer to the railway, and as it got closer, it became more and more unsettling. No one had ever heard anything like it. It didn't take long for the four men to huddle together, talking and listening, scared to death.

When the sound got close enough that they were sure it wasn't human, they fled. Not one of them stayed long enough to even fire a shot. They were soon back at camp.

There wasn't much anyone in camp could do, as it was too dark and the worksite too distant. Everyone discussed the howling, as many of those in camp had also been awakened by it. It was as strange and weird a sound as anyone had ever heard, and a few of the men wanted to leave camp the next day, but were talked into staying.

Now the boss had to rethink his strategy. Every bit of work they were doing was being undone each night. They had made zero progress, and they had no explanation for why, except someone was tearing up their work as fast as they could do it. And it was strange, as it would take as many guys to tear it up as to put it down, but there were no tracks or signs of activity.

It was going to be hard to explain this to the higher ups, who were already pressuring them to make fast work because of the competition for the coal markets. It was likely some heads would roll.

The next day, nobody went to work. It was a hopeless situation until they could solve what was going on. Everyone enjoyed the day off, but they also knew they wouldn't get paid. Some of the guys were stewing on this and decided it had something to do with the Chinese workers, that they were in on it somehow, and they started in on them, but this was quickly shut down by the boss. He knew he had a crisis brewing.

That night, guards were again set, as the boss knew the destruction would continue, even though they hadn't laid new track that day. There was plenty of old track to rip out. Nobody wanted the job of sitting out there at night, and threatening to fire them didn't work, as they all wanted to leave anyway.

So, the boss had to sweeten the pot by offering to pay double wages before he could get anyone out there. My great-grandpa Will was again one of those who volunteered. He wanted the money to go start his own ranch someday.

So there Will sat, along with two others, the only ones the boss could get to go out there. At this point, they all hung together, as nobody had the guts to sit out there alone.

There was a half moon, and it wasn't long before Will could see something walking up the already laid tracks. It suddenly dawned on him that this was why there hadn't been any tracks, they were staying on the rails! But how could they stay on the rails and tear them up? They had to be really agile, lifting the rails ahead of them.

He pointed this out to the others, and they all sat there silently, not sure what to do. Now they could hear talking, and sure enough, it sounded like Chinese, yet it somehow didn't. Will had been around the Chinese guys quite awhile and had even learned a little of the language, and he really didn't think this was Chinese. Maybe it was Japanese, he thought, though that didn't make sense.

But when the figures got closer, they could see they weren't humans at all! There were two of them, and sure enough, they started tearing up the rails. The three men were now hidden behind the rocks watching, afraid to move.

The creatures were eight to nine feet tall and had to weigh at least 600 pounds each, with shoulders twice as wide as a large man's. And as they tore up the rails, they grunted and made deep sounds kind of like a mixture of a bear and a monkey, but they sometimes stopped and chattered in what sounded a bit like Japanese.

They stood on the rails behind the ones they were tearing up, and the sheer power exhibited by these beasts was incredible as they ripped things up, twisting the rails and tossing them like matchsticks. They seemed to be very angry.

That was all it took for Will and the others to get out of there. They got back to camp as quickly as possible and woke up the boss, telling him what they'd seen. By morning, the entire camp was aware of what had happened, and many of the men were leaving, along with Will, in spite of the protests of the boss. It was all over.

I don't know if the boss and those who stayed tried to keep going, but I do know the railroad eventually gave up on building that spur, saying it was too expensive to continue. It's there in the history books, but very few know the real story as to why it was too expensive. That spur was under construction for only one year, from 1881 to 1882.

It's interesting that we use the term "monkey wrenching" to describe exactly the type of activity those Bigfoot were engaged in. And if Bigfoot are from the ape family, well, then the term really fits.

I never met my great-grandpa Will, but my dad says he was an honest and good man. My dad also said that after this experience, my great-grandpa left the railroad and started working on a ranch in Wyoming, where he met his future wife, my great-grandmother, Elsie, and eventually was able to homestead his own ranch land.

One time, my dad and I went out past Green River on what's called the Green River Cutoff, where all of this happened. There is still lots of railroad stuff around. The grade is easy to follow, and there are still ties here and there, and in some places, some pretty good piles, though the wood is all weathered and gray.

We found a couple of old roofless shelters made of ties, and also some stone shelters. I have three railroad spikes that I took home in memory of my great-grandpa.

So, I guess I have to thank the Bigfoot for my life, as my great-grandparents would never have met if Will had continued working on the railroad.

I guess that gives one a new perspective on things, being thankful to a Bigfoot for being born. Life never ceases to amaze me.

[13] Dirt Biking
with Uncle Hairy

· ·

I first met Brad when he came to a talk I was giving for an old-timers club who wanted to learn more about flyfishing. He was a younger guy and had brought his dad and just sat in the back, seeming pretty disinterested. But afterwards, he asked me about my expeditions. I thought it was kind of strange at the time, as he asked me how safe they were and if you had to fish alone.

Well, he ended up coming out for a few days flyfishing with his dad and seemed to really enjoy it. I finally asked him if he'd thought fishing was a dangerous sport, and in answer, he said he just didn't like being outdoors alone in the backwoods. When I looked puzzled, he told me this story, which made everything clear. —Rusty

It's funny how things get started, and then one thing leads to another, then you're having an adventure you never dreamed you'd have. And in my case, it was an adventure I never want to have again, I can tell you that.

It all started with an add on Craigslist that read some-thing like, "Dirt bike, super deal, wife says it must go or I am gone."

I was 17 and had been wanting a dirt bike since forever, but I didn't have the cash to buy one. But as I sat there in front of my mom's computer longingly admiring the photo of the blue Yamaha 250, my dad just happened to walk by and saw it, too.

"How much they want?" he asked.

"It's only $1200, a real deal, Dad."

I think my dad was having a momentary flashback to his youth, because he never bought me anything, he always made me work for whatever I wanted, except the basics, of course. And that meant I didn't have much, because who can make much money at 17? I had tried the McDonald's gig, but it started interfering with my homework, so my mom made me quit.

"You get straight A's the rest of the school year and I'll get you one just like it," my Dad promised.

Man, talk about a motivator! I was going into my last part of high school, and I guess my dad wanted me to quit screwing around. I knew it was too late for a good scholar-ship to college, as my grades were OK, but not stellar, but I guess my dad wanted me to go out with a bang.

And I did, in more ways than one. I worked really hard, got straight A's (I don't think my dad really expected that), and I was soon the proud owner of a used Honda 250. My mom then took me into the bike shop and bought me a helmet, boots, and some knee and elbow guards. Man, I was all set up and ready to go. I guess they were considering it my graduation present. Some kids get cars, I got a dirt bike, and I was happier than if it had been a Mustang.

I was ready to hit the trails, but I didn't have enough experience to really ride anything much, so I started riding at the edge of town, which backed up to a bunch of hills with old roads where the kids did BMX and people rode their ATVs.

I worked myself around on that and was soon doing pretty good, so I headed out on some longer backroads around town. This was in western Colorado, not far out of the little town of Fruita, and there were plenty of backroads. It was a biker's paradise, endless desert to ride.

I guess my dad was kind of regretting buying me the bike along about mid-June, because I hadn't yet got a job, I'd been too busy riding. I needed money to start school that fall, as I planned to go to a nearby technical college that taught automotive and diesel mechanics, which is what I figured I'd do.

Well, when I wasn't out riding, I was hanging around the bike shop, and that's where I met Cody. Cody was a year older than me and worked there, doing some sales and office work. She was an avid rider and had even raced some, so she became my mentor. We became good friends and started riding together on the weekends. I learned quite a bit about dirt biking from her, and she helped me get a part-time job in the shop, working on bikes. That was too cool, and it made my parents happy.

Well, as the summer went on, I got to be a better rider, and one weekend Cody and I decided to really hit the big time, to go up in the Books, what everyone called the mountains that ranged the east side of the valley. They were actually called the Bookcliffs, and they had this mystique about them, as they were pretty big and yet were close enough to town that we could reach them, spend the day riding, then get back by dark.

We spent half of Friday there at the shop studying the maps, and found a road that looked pretty interesting. We would ride up this canyon where there were natural gas wells, then it looked like the road kind of climbed on up to the top. The canyon looked a bit steep and narrow, so we thought it might be a lot of fun, and when we got up on top, we could enjoy the views.

The next day, we were all set. We had packed lunches and water and everything we needed to head out. It looked like it was going to be a typical Colorado summer day, blue skies and warm. I was really excited. This would be my first real trip on the dirt bike. I felt pretty competent, having ridden some gnarly trails close to town and all, but I was glad Cody was with me.

I followed her out of town, then we turned off the pavement onto a well-maintained gravel road. Some oil and gas company had stuff up there, tanks and pump jacks, so they kept the road maintained. We took it easy, not wanting to throw gravel up and ding up our bikes. Ironic as heck, as we usually rode like bats out of hell when we were out in the dirt.

After a few miles, the road started up the canyon, and we were soon passing a few wellheads. Before long, the road narrowed and turned into dirt with no gravel. We had passed all the wells, and the road was no longer maintained, and I guessed it didn't see much use, just an occasional dirt biker or ATVer and a few hunters in season. We had to take it easy, as it became rutted and rough.

We were now climbing up the canyon, and the sagebrush became scrub oak, which got taller and bigger as we rode higher. Before long, as we continued climbing, we started to get into some small stands of what looked like pine and aspens.

Now the road was just one-lane and barely qualified as a road at all. After coming up a really steep section, we topped out and were in a pretty good forest of what looked like Douglas fir. It was nice and cool, and we stopped for a break in a little meadow. We were having a blast!

Only problem was, we couldn't see out at all. We sat there and ate a snack and had some water, then decided to keep going. For some reason, we were both wanting to get up where we could see out, maybe because we knew the views would be incredible. We had climbed several thousand feet, but we weren't anywhere near the highest point, even though we had topped out of the canyon and were now in an upland area.

I knew the Books had plenty of black bears, so I was kind of keeping an eye out, but not a bit worried, as they're generally afraid of people. It's a wild area and has lots of backcountry I bet nobody ever sets foot in, except maybe an occasional hunter. The outdoorsy people tended to go up into the high mountains, like around Ouray and Aspen and those areas, and the Books really don't have many roads.

Once we got up on top, it was just forest, no big peaks to climb or cool trails for mountain biking, though that's changing now. But when this happened, hardly anyone ever went into the Books.

We continued on, and the road got better, a little wider, though still pretty rutted. We had decided to go on up, as the map showed the road continuing on up to the top of a 9,000 foot hill. To us Coloradoans, that's a hill, but I will say the road up there felt like we were going up a mountain. It's really rugged country.

Well, we crossed a big meadow, with aspens all around, and then we started climbing again. At this point, I can say we were way out there, and from the looks of the road, nobody had been on it for some time. It was pretty much grown over with grasses, but we could still make it out, even though it was starting to look more like a cow path.

Now it wound through the aspens, a true single track at this point. We had been through all kinds of terrain by now, and it felt like a real adventure. Little did I know how much more of an adventure we were soon to have.

Finally, after having to get off and move some fallen aspens from the trail, we reached the end, a small clearing, and we still weren't at the top. We had to get off and hike another tenth of a mile or so on up to a rocky point.

We grabbed our lunches and water and climbed on up, which didn't take very long. We were right, it was a view to die for, well almost to die for, because after I thought we might actually die up there, I wish I'd stayed home.

We sat there, eating our sandwiches, and we could see all the way into Utah in one direction, and clear over to the

San Juan Mountains in another, as well as high up onto the flanks of Grand Mesa. We were up so high you could actually make out the curvature of the earth.

What a place! We sat there, making out landmark mountains and such, and really enjoying ourselves. We were about as far from civilization as you can get without actually hiking into wilderness for miles and miles.

We had ridden a couple of hours to get there, but it was well worth it, even though my knees were getting a bit sore from all the obstacles we'd encountered, mostly logs. I was later glad for those logs, because the practice going over them gave me the courage and expertise to do what I had to do later.

It was going on mid-afternoon, and I noticed some clouds building up, so we decided to head on back, even though it didn't look like anything serious. We hiked back to the bikes and put our stuff away, then got on.

I was getting ready to start up when Cody held her hand up, like no, don't do anything. She looked at me and held her fingers to her lips to not talk, then kind of pointed in the direction she wanted me to look, trying not to be obvious about it.

There, standing right on the trail we had to go down, was something really big and dark. It just stood there, kind of in the shadows of the forest, where we really couldn't make out what it was, but we could tell it was big and it appeared to be standing on two legs. I felt suddenly chilled and very nervous.

I looked at Cody. Her face was white. Whatever it was, it was scaring her, too. I looked back at the shadows and the thing was still standing there. It hadn't moved at all. It was too big to be a black bear, and Colorado doesn't have any grizzlies.

But now, it began to sway back and forth, like a ghost. I think it knew we saw it and was trying to somehow hide itself. I whispered to Cody, asking her what she thought it was.

"I don't know," she replied. "But we have to get by it somehow, and it's too big. It could pick me up with one finger."

Well, that was bit of an exaggeration, but it was big, maybe seven feet tall, and massively built. It was hard to tell with it in the shadows, but it looked like it was completely covered in dark hair. But you could tell it was muscular and thick through the body.

I have no idea how long Cody and I sat there on our bikes, just watching. It was starting to get late afternoon, and the shadows were lengthening. We couldn't just sit there any longer. We had to get out and back before it got dark. We had lights on our bikes, but the road was just too rough and there were too many forks we'd taken. At night, it would be easy to miss a turn and get completely lost. But we seemed to be frozen in place.

This thing kept swaying, but then it turned and grabbed an aspen tree and literally wrenched it from the ground, throwing it across the path. The tree was probably a good fifteen feet tall, not a small one. Now our way out was blocked.

"What are we gonna do?" I kind of moaned to Cody. I didn't want her to think I was a coward, but I sure felt like one.

"We have to make a run for it," she replied. "A very good accurate run with no mistakes. Look, that log that thing threw down on the trail isn't really that big. Do you think you can jump it?"

"I dunno," I answered. I was still pretty wet behind the ears when it came to doing anything very technical on my bike. I'd tried a few jumps and such, but never anything much.

"We have to do this, Brad. You have to make that jump. You won't get a second chance. Stay right behind me and do what I do. If you crash, I'll turn around and come back. I won't leave you here. We'll both get out on my bike, so don't be afraid."

I knew Cody was trying to pump me up, and I knew if I didn't make it the first time there was no way she could save me if that thing wanted me for lunch.

"Look, Brad, when you get to the log, bend your knees and pull up on the handlebars, then lean back a bit, but not too far, make your arms kind of stiff, then flex them as you land. Remember that dirt bump we were practicing on? Same deal, just a little stiffer."

"OK," I answered. "Let's do it."

"And remember, be confident. That's the key."

I laughed a bit at the irony. Be confident while jumping a log right in front of some huge animal that probably wants to kill you.

We started our bikes, and as we did so, I watched the creature. It didn't move, but stood right next to the trail. I knew it meant to stop us. Why, I didn't know. Maybe it was just trying to scare us out of its territory, or maybe it had intentions of harming us. I'll never know.

Cody was gutsy, I admit that. Not only gutsy, but she had the experience to ride about anything. I was neither gutsy nor experienced. I was scared, and I just wanted to get this over with. The tension was killing me. I nodded that I was ready, and she took off with me close behind.

It was a good couple of hundred feet to where the Bigfoot stood, and by the time we got to it, we were both going pretty fast. We needed the speed to clear that log. Kelly went flying right up to it, pulled back, lifted her front wheel and slammed into the log with her real wheel, which put her right over it. I wasn't very far behind her, and it looked to me that she had also slammed into the Bigfoot, but I couldn't stop.

I did exactly as she had said, and I was soon over the log. I landed and started fishtailing, with dirt and rocks flying everywhere. I almost lost it, but managed to recover. I had no idea where Cody was at this point, but I knew she wasn't ahead of me.

Oh man, what to do? I went a hundred feet or so, then slowed down, trying to look over my shoulder without stopping or crashing. Just then, I heard Cody's bike making that stinging whining noise that two-stroke bikes make when they're being revved up, and then she was right beside me yelling "Go! Go!" and I just gunned it and took off, right behind her again.

We rode like bats out of hell, and didn't stop until we were far far down the mountain, clear down by the gas wells and back on the maintained road.

Cody pulled over, and I pulled up next to her. She took her helmet off and just sat there on her bike. I could see her hands were shaking.

"What happened back there?" I asked.

"I hit the damn thing." She pointed to her front fender, which was twisted around to where it almost brushed her tire.

I whistled.

"Man, you're lucky you weren't hurt. Do you think you injured it?"

"I think I might have, but it was so huge, it felt like I'd hit a wall. It knocked me and my bike down, and I just jumped up as fast as I could and got back on and took off. I didn't even look back. I have no idea if it was injured."

Cody was rubbing her left arm, and I asked if she was OK. She just nodded and took off.

We made it back to the bike shop, as that's where Cody had parked her car. She always left her bike at the shop, as her parents lived about ten miles away. I offered to drive her home, but she said she would be alright.

That night, I got a call from her. It was pretty late, and she said she couldn't sleep, that she needed to talk to me, and we just talked on the phone for a long time.

Cody had been the one with an up close and personal encounter, I had only seen the thing from a distance, as it was down on the ground with her and her dirt bike on top of it when I came blasting through, right behind her. She wanted to talk about what she'd seen, which we did. We talked half the night before she was able to settle down and go to sleep.

The next day, Cody came by the house and picked me up, and we went to a fast-food restaurant and talked some more. She didn't want to be outside at all. I noticed she had two black eyes and her arm was all swollen.

My dirt bike just sat in the garage after that, and I don't think Cody rode any more either. My parents were puzzled, but I told them I was too busy to ride. By the time school came, I sold it. I had lost all interest in riding, in fact, I had lost all interest in any kind of outdoors sports. All I wanted to do was hang out inside and read or watch TV.

Cody sold her bike, too, and went off to the state college in Fort Collins, and I lost touch with her. I went ahead with the mechanic course and ended up doing pretty well, eventually opening my own shop.

To this day, I have never been back up in the Books, though I do enjoy going out to the lake at the state park near town and fishing when I can. Like I said earlier, it's funny how you end up having adventures you never dreamed of, and that's one I never want to have again.

[14] Bearly Climbing

· ·

A good friend came fishing with me one sunny Colorado afternoon and brought his new brother-in-law, Luke, who used to be a technical climber. That's one sport that's never interested me, since I have a fear of heights, but Luke says that shouldn't stop anyone because you're so well-protected that it's hard to fall. I then found out he himself had fallen and almost died and thus quit the sport.

After fishing, we built a little fire and roasted hotdogs for a snack, then headed on home. But while we were sitting around eating, Luke told the following story. It's definitely not one like anything I've heard before. —Rusty

I used to be a climber back in my youth, but one small mistake put an end to that. After six broken bones and three months in a hospital, I lost interest in climbing. Some of my friends told me I should go back, that I shouldn't let fear defeat me, but I refused, and I will say that a couple of them are now dead from climbing accidents.

But just because I didn't want to climb any more, that didn't mean I didn't still want to be out in nature, go to the mountains, and camp. I still loved all that, and there was no way I was giving that up.

So, I continued to backpack and hike and hang out with my climbing buddies. I would help plan trips and do whatever I could to be a part of the team, and that sometimes meant being the first safety belay at the bottom of the climb. But after that, they did their thing and I did mine, which usually meant I did day hikes and explorations while they climbed.

I had climbed in Wyoming's Wind River Mountains many times before my accident, and I still love that area, so when my good friends Chris and Emma said they were putting together a small group to go climb, I jumped at the chance to go along.

We would pack up to the Cirque of the Towers and they would climb while I enjoyed the scenery and did some hiking. I had discovered the world of photography and wanted to go up there and take some photos. The Winds is a stunning place.

They had wrangled up two more friends to go, so that made five of us total. Since they were coming down from Seattle and I was living in Boulder at the time, we agreed to meet in the little town of Pinedale, Wyoming and spend our first night near there, making plans and checking gear and all that. We met at the Wind River Brewing Company, the western gateway to the Winds.

I think the brewing company was worth the trip in itself, with good food and even better brew. We talked awhile and got caught up on what we'd been doing since we last met, then headed out the road that led up to Big

Sandy Campground, a good 50 or so miles from town, with the last ten miles being pretty rough going. By the time we reached the campground, we were all totally beat, so we made a quick camp and crashed for the night.

This is the most common way into the Cirque of the Towers, which is a pretty famous climbing area, at the southern end of the range. The Winds are really rugged, and the Cirque is one of the more rugged areas there, a place where glacial action has carved cirques and kettles and hanging valleys. It's a breathtaking semi-circle of fifteen craggy peaks, all above 12,000 feet, and it offers some of the best alpine granite rock climbing in the U.S.

We got up the next morning and repacked our tents and gear, then headed up the trail. There were a lot of cars in the parking lot, but we really didn't see hardly anyone the whole trip. The Bridger Wilderness is a huge area and can accommodate a lot of backpackers. We started out at around 9,000 feet, heading for what's called Jackass Pass, a high mountain pass that's really tough going and climbs to 10,800 feet.

It's a long hike back in there, about nine miles one-way, but the first six miles were easy, pretty flat, following the Big Sandy River. We reached Big Sandy Lake, which is really pretty, and took a break there, then continued on.

One of the waiters at the brewing company was a climber in his free time, and he told us the lake has tons of black bears around. He also told us that the talk of the whole summer was about a black bear that had been seen climbing in the Cirque several times, and at one point, it was going up a pretty steep route which was rated a 5.1.

···142···

In climbing talk, any time you get to a 5.0 and above, you're talking technical climbing, where aid is necessary. Apparently that bear didn't read the climbing manual, because it was climbing without aid. People do climb some of the 5+ stuff without ropes and such, but they're doomed if they slip even once.

So, we took a break and talked about the climbing bear. I kind of hoped we would see it, as it would make some awesome photos. The lake is really pretty, and a precursor of what was to come, reflecting the big granite monoliths of Big Sandy Mountain, Haystack Mountain, Schiestler Peak, and Temple and East Temple Peaks.

Well, now for the fun part—Jackass Pass. Supposedly, it got its name because only a jackass could travel it, or maybe, in our case, a dumbass, because it's one heck of a pass. It's steep and rocky and a real trial when you're loaded down with a backpack. Actually, it would be bad enough without all that weight.

But it's worth it, especially when you top out and are now looking right into the maw of the Cirque of the Towers, a semicircle ridge of jagged peaks, including some with really cool names like War Bonnet and Wolf's Head. We could also see down to Lonesome Lake, where we would camp. I can't begin to describe this view. It's absolutely stunning— tundra, glaciers, and granite.

We headed down and set up camp, not too close to the lake, as you're not supposed to camp there in order to keep it pristine. We had a huge dinner of fajitas. We were deep in a place that felt like paradise. And we were late enough in the season, mid-September, that the infamous mosquitoes were all gone.

It would be only a matter of a few weeks until the first snows shut the place down. We knew it was possible for early snows to hit when we were there, but the lack of bugs and people made it worth the risk. I had been in here once the same time of year with a climbing buddy, back when I climbed, and we'd ended up wading out through two feet of snow.

Because the Cirque is high in the tundra and there aren't any trees to hang food from, we had brought along some bear-proof portable food storage containers, which added to our load but ensured we'd have something to eat if bears did come around. The bears in the Winds include grizzlies, and they're getting too used to humans.

We didn't want any encounters, although I was still hoping for that climbing bear the guy in town had mentioned. I had been there one year when the grizzlies were pretty bad, coming into camp and looking for food, but the guy at the brew pub had said this year they seemed to have backed off some. Maybe because the climbers were being fined if they left trash or food around, and the wildlife people were up there enforcing it.

There was one other party camped not too far away, and I ambled over and talked to them for a bit, but they hadn't seen any bears nor heard of the climbing bear. We all laughed about it, but I knew the waiter had been serious and wasn't pulling my leg.

My group was there to climb Pingora, the central tower in the Cirque and one of the more famous climbs. Pingora has ratings ranging from 5.2 to 5.11. It's not the highest, but is probably the most eye-catching peak in the ring of towering spires and has one of the easiest approaches.

Well, you would think I would've slept like a baby that night after hiking nine miles carrying a heavy pack, but I didn't. First off, I couldn't go to sleep, and when I finally did, I suddenly woke around midnight with a strange feeling of dread. I lay there, wondering if I were somehow having one of those premonitions people talk about, where they feel like something bad's going to happen and then it does. I wondered if I shouldn't tell everyone what I was feeling and tell them not to go climbing. But then, after some thought, I figured it was the thin air up there, the lack of oxygen.

I lay there, thinking like that, including recalling a story I heard once about someone having a premonition about some loved one dying in a plane crash and telling them not to go, and sure enough the plane crashed and they would've died.

I then heard a deep sigh, like some really big animal nearby. Uh oh, bear, was my first thought, hoping it wasn't a grizzly. I lay there really still, wondering if anyone else was awake. I made sure my bear spray was nearby, then tried to relax and listen. Was I just exhausted and my mind playing tricks or was it really something?

Next, I heard something walking around camp, circling the perimeter of our tents, which we'd set up like a circled wagon-train out in the wilderness. The feeling of dread got heavier—that's the only way I know to describe it.

As I lay there, I could now hear whatever it was making the strangest sound I've ever heard. It's like it was talking to itself, but in a really soft whispering noise. I don't know what to compare it to except the sound a monkey makes, only deeper and huskier.

I turned over onto my side to try to listen better, and all of a sudden, I felt really groggy and wanted nothing more than to sleep, but all my senses said I had to stay awake or I would die.

Have you ever driven when you were so tired you knew you were a hazard, but you kept going? Like, you would pinch yourself, turn on the radio, open the windows, anything to wake up, and you knew you would die if you nodded off, but you were so groggy it was like you were dreaming? That's what I felt like.

I managed to stay awake, and the whispering sound was now returned by something further out from camp. It was like they were talking to each other, whatever they were. I then heard something actually scrape by my tent, brushing it as they went by. I was still groggy, but the terror of being eaten by a grizzly was enough to keep me awake. I recalled the previous summer when a guy camped in a primitive campground in Yellowstone was killed by a grizzly.

The last thing I remembered was hearing something making a forlorn howling out away from camp quite a ways, and it sounded like a mixture of wolf and human, like something from a Lon Cheney werewolf movie. It gave me chills and terrified me, but I could no longer stay awake and went to sleep.

The next morning, about five a.m., I was wakened by everyone getting up to go climb. You know how it is when you first wake up after something bad's happened the previous day—you know something's wrong, but your mind hasn't remembered exactly what it is yet, then after a moment you remember and it's like, oh crap!

Well, for a moment, I sort of luxuriated in not having to get up and in being able to just laze around and sleep in. Of course, having been a climber, I knew my friends would be rewarded when they reached the summit, but I was happy to spend the day hiking and taking photos. I no longer needed that adrenaline rush or feeling of accomplishment.

But then I suddenly set straight up in my bag, remembering the events of the previous night. The chill came back and I got up, not wanting to be alone in camp, deciding I would hike with them to Pingora. But it was too late, they were long gone.

I got up and made some coffee. I was scared stiff with it still being dark and everyone gone, and I even thought about packing up and heading back to the car. Instead, I just sat there, wrapped up in my down coat against the night chill until the sun finally came up.

I could now see over to the other camp, and it was empty also, as they were going to climb the face of Warbonnet, a tougher climb than Pingora. I had the valley all to myself, and I would normally be really relishing that, but now it felt ominous.

As the sun came up and everything looked more normal, I gradually began to feel better. I didn't want to sit around all day worrying, so I got my daypack, put in some snacks and water and camera gear, then headed out. I would just wander around, climb up the slopes a bit from the valley, and take photos. I was beginning to feel more normal. I was in one of the most stunning landscapes on Earth, and I should enjoy it.

I headed for Pingora. I wanted to hike around its base to get a good view of Wolf's Head, a big massif of granite that was another famous climb. The morning was chilly with clear skies, and I hoped to also see my friends on Pingora and get some photos for them to check out later. I wanted to be close to them, as I felt really unsettled.

I headed out, and the movement made me feel better, got the blood going a bit. I was analyzing the previous night, and I would swear we'd been visited by a bear except for the whispering and the weird howl, which mystified me. I had nary a clue what that could be.

I gradually worked my way to the base of Pingora, but over towards the side where a rough rocky valley went on up to Wolf's Head. I stopped to take some photos, and I was close enough that I could see Pingora really well, and I thought I saw climbers.

I pulled my Nikon high-powered binoculars from my pack and started watching them. Sure enough, it was my buddies. I could tell from the number in the group and the bright red jacket that Emma always wore. They had made really good progress and looked like they were doing well.

I took off my pack and sat down on a big rock, getting comfortable. I wanted to get more photos, plus I really felt unmotivated and tired.

As I sat there, scanning the face of Pingora with my binocs, something caught my eye, something way over to the left of my group, also on Pingora, climbing. Must be someone else climbing that we hadn't met, I thought, wondering where they had camped. I looked closer.

It appeared to be just one person, a solo climber, and they were all dressed in brown and bulky. The best climb-

ers tend to be small and wiry, though there are excep-
tions, and this guy looked like a big exception. And man,
he was hauling ass right up that route, really moving. It
then dawned on me that he was free-climbing, something
that gives me the chills. I wanted to stop watching, but I
couldn't. The last thing I wanted to see was someone fall to
their death.

Whoever this was, he was the best climber I'd ever seen.
His motions were fluid and smooth and he climbed like a
monkey.

Before long, he wasn't that far from my friends, and I
glassed them and could see they had stopped. Apparently
they also saw this guy climbing. I could imagine what they
must have thought, this big burly guy free-climbing not far
from them and going straight up that wall like it was nothing.

I thought for a moment about the climbing bear and
wondered...nah, no way a bear could climb like that, and
this guy was on a route that looked way harder than a 5.1. I
took some photos, but later when I saw them I was disappointed, as my 300 mm lens wasn't long enough to really
capture much, it just looked like a big guy climbing. But
those photos at least prove that I didn't make up the darn
thing.

For awhile it looked like the guy was angling over to my
friends, which I thought was kind of strange, but maybe he
was following a crack or something. Emma and everyone
had completely stopped climbing and were just watching
this guy, from what I could make out.

He wasn't too far from them when I heard that same howling I'd heard last night, and it was coming from this guy! That was too weird for me. Of course, your mind tries to make things logical, and I thought, what the heck was this big guy doing messing around our camp last night? Not cool. What I thought later was simply how close we'd been to a Sasquatch and what a scary yet unique event it had been. But at the time, my mind couldn't register what I was seeing.

Now the guy was climbing even faster and was soon gone, over the top of Pingora. I was shocked. No human could possibly climb so easily and so fast.

Now my friends were rappelling down off the face, coming down pretty fast. They had decided not to finish their climb. I couldn't see where this guy had gone, but I was worried he was coming down the back side and might come right around my way, as it was the route back to the valley. I picked up my gear and took off back to camp. When I got there, I started packing up. There was no way I was going to stay, even if I had to hike out alone.

It was a couple of hours before my friends got back, early afternoon, and they were a pretty shook up bunch. Nobody said much, they just started packing up camp. They were ready to go, too.

By the time they were ready to head out, the other climbers had returned, so I went over to talk to them. They'd had a successful climb and were high as kites. I told them about the previous night and what we'd seen, but they thought I was kidding, I guess, because they didn't seem to let it phase them. We said our goodbyes, and my group and I headed out.

Climbing back up Jackass Pass was grueling for my friends, as they'd just climbed part of Pingora, but we made good time, no one saying a word. I kept looking behind us, worried we might be followed, but I never saw anything.

We got back to our vehicles, then piled in and headed for Pinedale, where we got spaces in an RV park. I think it was the first time any of us had ever stayed in an RV park, but it seemed pretty darn nice, being surrounded by people. I didn't even mind the sounds of generators and barking dogs and kids yelling, it all kind of comforted me. Normally, I would move camp if I could even see anyone in the distance, and my friends were the same.

We ended up back at the brewery for dinner, and that same waiter served us, surprised to see us back so soon. I told him we'd seen the climbing bear, but it wasn't a bear. He just laughed. He'd known all along, but didn't believe it. But I think our recounting of the day's events may have helped change his mind.

Anyway, that was my last visit into the Winds. Between my knees starting to hurt after long hikes and the climbing "bear," I've lost interest in doing anything but lowland desert hikes, and then in moderation.

After I got home, I got on the internet and checked things out. I actually found a reference to that climbing "bear" on a rock climbing site, so I knew we weren't the only ones who had seen it. But on the other hand, there were also some threads about actual bears being able to climb up to a 5.7, which kind of blew my mind.

In any case, I hope that climbing "bear" was just out having a good day and never crashes and burns like I did.

[15] Squaw Lake
· ·

This story was told by a fellow from Phoenix, Arizona, who had come up to fish the waters of the Big Hole River in Montana, one of my favorite places. I thought it was a great story, and it underscored how sometimes you're not very scared of things that maybe you should be. But if you don't know what they are in the first place, well, maybe ignorance is bliss. —Rusty

I once had a dream of hiking the entire length of the Pacific Crest Trail, all 2,663 miles, from the Mexican border to the Canadian border. It's an unbelievable hike, and I'd done several stretches of it at the time this story took place.

I was in my 40s and looking for a challenge that went beyond all the wild things I'd done in my youth, something I could look back at with pride. Maybe I was fighting off the thought of becoming middle-aged, I don't know.

I'd come across a copy of a book by Eric Ryback, the seventeen year-old who claimed to be the first to hike the trail as a thru-hiker, which means he did it all without stopping or doing sections one at a time. Eric claimed to have set up intricate resupply packages and said he often went hungry. He was later accused of having taken car rides, so I don't know if his story is true, but it inspired me to want to do that hike.

So there I was, visiting my sister, who lived in Klamath Falls, Oregon, for a week in July of 1987. She has since moved, and I haven't been back to that country for years, as I live in Phoenix.

It was a nice summer day, my sis was at work, and I wanted to go check out a section of the Pacific Crest trail that ran not too far from town. There were several places I could intersect it and hike it as far as I wanted to go.

I had studied the maps and set up my daypack the previous day, and I was all set to go. I decided on going to the Four Mile Lake area, which was about 35 miles northwest of Klamath Falls on the highway, then another six miles on a dirt road that led to Four Mile Lake Campground.

As I drove up that so-called dirt road, I realized it wasn't the kind of dirt I'm used to at all, but was made of cinders. I was in volcano country. I could see the huge peak of Mt. McLoughlin towering over everything ahead of me, the highest peak in southern Oregon, and it for sure looked like a volcano.

I parked my old Nissan pickup there at the campground, in the shade of a big Lodgepole pine, then started out on the trail. There was no one around, which surprised me, as it was such a nice day, even though it was midweek. I did see a small older VW Rabbit parked nearby, but with nobody in or around it. Probably another hiker, I figured. It's a small and very pretty campground, so I'm sure it fills up on the weekends.

Four Mile Lake is pretty darn big, especially for someone from Phoenix, where a lake is a rare sight. It sits right
under Mt. McLoughlin, which I would stake my life on
being a cinder cone volcano, just like its neighbor down the
road a ways, Mt. Shasta. Even though it was July, the slopes
of the mountain had snow partway down them. It was a
very picturesque and beautiful place, the lake and that big
mountain towering a good 4,000 feet above it.

I started out on a trail called the Sky Lakes Wilderness
Trail that wound through a dense fir forest filled to the gills
with mosquitoes. I was ready for them, though, as I had my
bug net, the same one I used around Phoenix to keep off
the gnats. I had been warned by my sister, and I also wore
long pants and a long-sleeved cotton shirt. They didn't
bother me, but they sure tried.

After about three miles of pretty easy hiking, I came to
Squaw Lake, a smaller lake not far from Four Mile Lake.

Several social trails took off to Squaw Lake from the
main trail, probably created by fisherman. I wasn't in any
hurry, so I decided to take one of them and go see what the
lake looked like. I'd been hiking for three miles, and I was
ready for a break.

I was soon at the lakeshore, and I found a nice rock to
sit on, where I drank some water and ate a granola bar. As I
was sitting there, I noticed movement not too far down the
lakeshore from where I sat. There was someone else here,
and I figured it was whoever owned the VW Rabbit.

They hadn't seen me, so I just sat there and watched
them to see what they were doing, as they were walking
back and forth along the shoreline. They had something on

their back that kind of looked like a pack, but not quite, and I wasn't close enough to make it out.

As I sat there, this figure stopped walking back and forth and just stood there for a bit, then started walking out into the water. It seemed to me that it the water would be a bit cold to be swimming, and it didn't look like they were wearing swimming gear, but rather were totally clothed, so I found this strange.

What was even stranger was the fact that they disappeared into the water, not swimming at all, but just walked into it and disappeared. This alarmed me, and I wondered if someone were trying to commit suicide or something. I stayed there for a long time, searching the waters with my eyes, trying to see if a body surfaced somewhere in the vicinity, but nothing came up. The figure just disappeared.

I wasn't sure what to do. I hadn't seen a ranger or anyone, and by the time I got back to report it, the person would be beyond help. In fact, they were probably already drowned, I figured, as I'd been sitting there a good fifteen minutes watching for them.

Maybe they'd swam underwater and come up along the shore where I couldn't see them. I finally stood up and headed back to the trail, having decided to go ahead with my hike, as I didn't know what else to do.

I hiked on up until I started getting into what appeared to be a hemlock forest. Before too long, I was really climbing, and the hemlocks began to make way for gnarled pines and manzanita. I could see the flanks of Mt. McLoughlin through the trees, and it looked to me like there was a crater on its flanks left by a lateral volcanic blast, but I had read it was really a terminal glacial moraine, a fact verified when the trail met the rubble field at its bottom.

It was a beautiful place, but I was still thinking about the person who had walked into the lake, and wondering if they were OK.

It was then that I had a strange feeling that I was being followed. I turned and scoped out the trail, but didn't see anyone. I continued on, but my senses were at high alert, and for no particular reason, as I hadn't heard or seen anything. It was hard to explain to myself, as I'm a pretty pragmatic person, but I somehow knew I wasn't alone up there.

Not long after I started getting that feeling, I heard something in the thick shrubs alongside the trail, but back in maybe thirty or forty feet, not really close. I stopped and strained to see into the shadows, but saw nothing, and the noise had stopped. It was like someone was walking alongside the trail and stepping on branches and breaking them.

The noise started up when I did, and when I would stop, it stopped. I started getting an uncontrollable feeling of terror, something I've never felt before, and I've been out with coyotes and bears and even charged by javelinas. On top of all this, I was getting tired, as I wasn't in top shape, so I decided to go back.

I wanted to run, but I knew if it was a predator, that was a bad idea, so I just hiked back down at a really fast pace. Whatever it was, it had turned with me and was still paralleling the trail. As I got back down a ways, I noticed some big branches had been broken off nearby trees and laid across the trail. It had to have been done very recently, as I knew they weren't there when I came up.

Now, as I got further back down, this thing started making a noise that I can only describe as being bird-like, in that it was like a bird call, although not quite. It was high and shrill and like a hoot, but more drawn out. This wasn't anything I'd ever heard, and I couldn't figure how a bear could make a sound like that.

I was now worried I was being followed by someone who maybe wanted to rob me or something, as it sounded like a person walking alongside me, someone big enough to be able to crash through thick underbrush. All I had for protection was a pocket Leatherman tool, which wasn't much. And now I thought maybe the bird call was a signal to someone else. I was extremely nervous and really wanted to run.

I was soon back to Squaw Lake, where I decided to step off the trail and go down to the lake to the shoreline, where I could be out in the open more and away from the underbrush. I went down by the water and stood there, looking back into the trees and wondering if whoever it was would come out where I could see them.

I hung out there for a good half-hour and saw nothing. I also needed some time to rest, which was another reason for going down there. I now remembered the guy who had walked into the lake and again wondered what had happened.

I sat on another rock and scanned the lakeshore, but didn't see a soul. It had been a couple of hours since I'd been there before, and nothing looked any different.

I was finally feeling better and getting ready to leave, when that same figure walked out of the lake, almost in the same spot it had gone in. It just emerged like some creature covered with moss in a monster movie. I just sat there and watched, wondering what the heck was going on.

Now the figure took off the backpack thing and slung it over its arm, then sat down and took something off its feet and appeared to be putting on shoes. It began walking towards me.

As it got closer, I could see it was a tall thin man wearing a wetsuit and carrying oxygen dive tanks, and that made me sigh a sigh of relief. Who would expect someone to be diving out here, especially in these cold waters? I was very happy to have some company on the trail back down, so I waited for him to come closer, then I greeted him and introduced myself.

His name was Bob and he was very friendly, and I asked him if the water was cold. He said it was, but the wetsuit made it tolerable. We talked for a bit, then I asked what was down there that someone would want to dive in cold water to see. He looked at me kind of like he was checking me out, then said he had a theory he was trying to prove, but he knew I would think he was crazy, so he really didn't want to talk about it.

Well, there's no better way to make someone curious than to say something like that. I assured him I wouldn't think he was crazy, but he didn't need to share it unless he felt comfortable.

He laughed, then told me that this was Bigfoot country, and a friend of his had been fishing and watched a Bigfoot walk straight into the water and not come back out. So now he was here trying to see if there was any chance these creatures lived in underwater caves, which would explain why nobody could ever find them.

It would be a good hiding place, and since this was a volcanic area, maybe there were lava tubes or such under there that led up above water level so the Bigfoot would have oxygen and also a good safe home. Bob had been a diver in the Navy, so he was comfortable underwater.

Well, I did think he was crazy, but I just agreed that it made sense and didn't tell him I thought Bigfoot was an urban legend (or maybe a non-urban legend would make more sense). As we sat there, he told me more about Bigfoot, which, being from the southwest, wasn't part of my cognitive mindset.

Apparently, Squaw Lake had been the site of a number of Bigfoot encounters, especially among fishermen. He hadn't seen one himself, but he did believe in them, and he was sure he'd been followed by them more than once.

As he talked, a sense of realization came over me, and I wondered if that wasn't exactly what had been following me. My disbelief was beginning to be challenged. I told Bob what had happened up the trail, and he got a look of consternation.

"Maybe we better head out," he said, nervously looking into the forest.

I agreed, and we headed out. We were soon back on the main trail, and only had three miles to go until we reached the campground. We'd gone maybe a half mile, neither of us taking our time, when a scream pierced the air and echoed through the thick forest. It was unreal, and started out like a cow bellowing, then turned into a shriek like a banshee from hell.

How can you adequately describe a sound like that? It's impossible, and the effect it has on one is unlike anything a normal person ever experiences. All I can say is that it was really loud, really echoey, and really terrifying. Whatever made it sounded mad, and it sounded like it wasn't far behind us.

Well, Bob started running, and I was right behind him, his wetsuit making a whish whish sound. We were both running for our lives. Now a big branch crashed right next to us, and I wasn't going to turn around to see what had thrown it.

Bob must've been in pretty good shape, because, wetsuit or not, he was soon way ahead of me and out of sight. This kind of irritated me because I didn't think it was cool to leave someone in a situation like we were in. I figured we should stick together. Apparently Bob thought otherwise.

I had run maybe a good half-mile when I started getting a hitch in my side. I wasn't a runner, I was barely a hiker, and a slow hiker at that. I had to stop, as I was starting to hurt, and I couldn't breathe. I stepped off the trail and behind a big tree and leaned against it, panting, certain this was the end.

It sounds kind of funny when you tell it, but after hearing that scream, believe me, it was terrifying. I read later that Bigfoot is pretty harmless in general, there haven't been many accounts of actual harm, but it's very territorial and will scare you to death. I think that's what was going on.

I heard something really really big crashing through the brush on the other side of the trail from me, and it just went on by. Was it possible it hadn't seen me? I was huffing and puffing so hard it was difficult to even think straight, but I hoped so.

All was now quiet and I'd regained my composure a bit. What to do? If I just went on down the trail, odds are good I would eventually encounter it again.

I could see Four Mile Lake through the trees, and I decided to get down to the shoreline and hike back that way, as the campground sat right on the lake, in fact, when the lake was high, the campground was flooded. That way I could stay completely off the trail.

I worked my way through the thick brush and trees, with every little sound setting off my heart, thinking it was the Bigfoot. But I was finally over by the lake, and I just followed the shoreline back. When I arrived at the campground, the VW Rabbit was gone, and several of the picnic tables had been turned over, which would be no easy task.

I slunk over to my pickup and slipped inside, locking the doors, then started up and took off. I just gunned it and bounced down the road as fast as I could get that old pickup going.

I have no idea who Bob was, but I assume he made it out OK, since his car was gone. I at first thought he was pretty brave, diving down looking for Bigfoot caves, but in retrospect, he wasn't one of the braver fellows I've met. He sure was out for saving himself.

If I hadn't slipped off the trail, I have no idea what would've happened. That was enough of Oregon hiking for me, and I spent the rest of my time there reading about Bigfoot on the internet, feeling glad I lived in Phoenix.

[16] Old Brown

· ·

I love fishing the Williams Fork River, and the old school in this story still stands along its banks, last I was there. I've been by it many times and fished near it with no idea of its history.

I know I'll have a different perspective on the area after hearing this story, which was told by a guy who now runs a ranch there that he inherited. He told me there's never been any sign of Old Brown since the day he was run off, and most of the people around the area are totally unaware of what happened. He said he hopes Old Brown never comes back, and I have to agree, as I don't like sharing my fish with someone who would think of a big five-pound trout as mere finger food. —Rusty

My dad told me this story when I was just a kid, and it scared the crap out of me. It actually made me afraid to go out in the woods alone. One day, years after he had told it, I mentioned the effect it had on me, and he said he was very sorry to have scared me.

We talked about it for a long time, and I'm convinced he was being honest about what happened. He was a very straightforward man with a lot of integrity. He did say he knew these creatures were real, and maybe he had told me the story out of concern for my safety, although unintentionally scaring me. Anyway, here's the story, and I'll just tell it like I remember him telling it.

My dad went to school in a one-room schoolhouse. Since he was born in 1930, I would guess this happened in about 1940, as he said he was in fifth or sixth grade. That would make him around eleven or twelve years old. Not so young that he couldn't recall it pretty clearly.

The schoolhouse sat on a piece of land, maybe an acre, that had been donated by a local rancher who wanted a place to send his kids to school. The locals had built the school, and it was just a single room with a big woodstove and about ten desks, maybe fifteen, but not a lot. It had a little back room for storing wood, as well as being a place for the kids to take off their coats and boots. This was also the entrance.

The school had been built from local wood, probably some kind of pine from higher up in the mountains. The school sat near a tiny town called Hamilton, which had maybe thirty residents and was positioned at the bottom of a small valley where the Williams Fork River flowed through. I think the town has actually lost most of its residents in the past 30 years or so.

This was in northwestern Colorado, which is mostly sagebrush and canyon country, with uplands having lots of scrub oak and then aspens and pine higher up. There are mountains, but they're not the jagged kind you see in other parts of the state, but mostly just giant hills with rugged terrain. Few people ever went up into the hills, except to hunt, and I think it's still that way.

This was ranching country, with the lowlands along the river used for hayfields and winter pasture and the higher country, up in the aspens, used for summer grazing. But there weren't a lot of ranches, as it took a lot of land to make a go of it.

The town kids walked to school, but the ranch kids all rode horses, and there was a small corral near the school building. The kids would take the horses down to the nearby river for water. The Williams Fork isn't a big river, but more like a large wide stream and pretty shallow in most places. I used to inner tube it as a kid when I'd go visit my grandparents' ranch.

Anyway, my dad and his younger sister, who everyone called "the Kid," rode to school every day on an old quarter horse they had named Nollie, who was old and pretty much retired, except to haul the kids around. The ranch was about two miles up the road from the school. These ranch kids were pretty tough and used to doing things on their own since they were little, and they sure weren't coddled.

My dad said that one day, in the spring, he and the Kid had just come into the little inner room of the school and were taking off their boots when a little town girl came in and was scared and crying. My dad asked her what was wrong, and she said there was big gorilla in the willows by the river watching her, and it had followed her to school.

My dad went outside and looked around, but didn't see anything. As he was out there, the teacher, Miss Thomas, came out. The little girl had told her the same story. They looked around, but neither of them saw a thing.

My dad always took Nollie down to the river for a drink before the ride home, and he said that later that afternoon when school was out, when he tried to take her down there, she wouldn't go. He figured she wasn't thirsty, though that was unusual for her.

He went back up to the school and got the Kid, then the pair started for the ranch. They rode double down the dirt road that went through the valley and paralleled the thick willows along the river.

As they were riding along, all of a sudden Nollie just took off with them, kind of a runaway, heading for the ranch. She had never done this before, and there was nothing my dad could do to get her to stop. She took them right up to the door of the ranch house, when normally they would go to the barn and unsaddle her, let her out to pasture, then walk to the house.

My grandma was there and wondered why Nollie was so lathered up. The kids weren't supposed to ride her hard, since she was old. My dad told my grandma what had happened, but he neglected to mention the big gorilla at the school, as he had forgotten all about it.

Nollie wanted to stay up at the house, close to them, and they couldn't get her back to the barn. So my grandma just unsaddled here there and gave her some water and let her graze on the lawn. She would let my grandpa deal with it when he got in from the fields, where he'd been checking on some cattle that were calving.

Well, when he came in, Nollie was fine and he put her out to pasture. They had no idea what had been wrong, but later that night, they got an inkling when the cattle started making a commotion.

Calving season is the worst time for ranchers, as the cows often need assistance and predators can be a problem. It can be a grueling and sleepless time. When my grandpa heard the cattle carrying on, he grabbed his rifle and a spotlight and headed out for the pasture. He knew either coyotes or a cougar were in the area for the cattle to act like that.

The first thing he noticed was the strong odor. It smelled like something indescribable and made him want to throw up. It was really strong, and it was coming from the direction of the cows.

He had his cowdogs, Lucy and Sam, with him, and when they got to the pasture gate, they turned around and high-tailed it back to the house. This was a first for them, as they were usually the ones that took off chasing, and they'd even chased off a cougar once.

My grandfather stopped and thought about this. It made him nervous, so he got his rifle and fired off a few rounds into the air, then proceeded to go see what was going on.

As he started in, here came the cattle, pretty much stampeding, and this was bad, as some had tiny calves that no way could keep up with them.

My grandfather went back to the house and got my dad and my uncle, as he needed reinforcements. They all had flashlights, and they went out into the pasture and started walking around, seeing what was going on and looking for calves.

After a bit, the cattle all started coming back around, and the moms were reunited with their calves, who were bawling their heads off by then. It looked like everyone was there and OK, except the excitement had caused one cow to go into labor, and she looked like she was having a hard time.

My dad went back inside, but his older brother stayed out to help. Pulling a calf is hard work, and if they had to take this route, my grandfather could use his help.

Well, it wasn't long before the calf was born, and they had taken it and the mom into the barn for the night where Nollie was. They were pretty tired by then, so they came back into the house. The dogs were hiding under the kitchen table and couldn't be coaxed out, no matter what, which was worrisome. There had to be something out there, as they never acted like this.

The rest of the night went OK, and nothing unusual happened. My grandfather went out a couple of times to check on everything, and the second time the dogs went along and everything was fine.

The next day, my dad and the Kid set off for school on Nollie, and it was as if nothing had happened. When they got to school, they could smell something awful, and the teacher remarked on it, wondering if anyone had any idea what it could be. It smelled like something dead, only one-hundred times as strong.

By lunch, the smell was gone, and the kids all went out into the school yard to eat their sack lunches, and the ones with horses would lead them down for water. There were no problems until it was time to go back in for the afternoon, and that's when my dad said he saw something big and black down in the willows.

Now, Hamilton really isn't bear country, as it's high desert. It's more like rattlesnake country and has rock cliffs above it that are home to these snakes that sometimes come into town. I actually was riding my bike there once and ran next to what I thought was a stick and had a rattler strike my bike pedal. But bears, no way, it was too low and hot.

But my dad thought what he saw in the willows was a bear, and he yelled for everyone to get inside and then went running in to tell the teacher. He was the oldest kid in the school, and the teacher sometimes relied on him for help with things like bringing in wood and helping with the younger kids.

Miss Thomas made sure everyone was inside, then carefully looked out the window. The horses were running around the corral, all frantic, and she knew there was something wrong, but there wasn't much she could do about it. This was long before cell phones, and she didn't even have a regular phone.

The kids were too excited to do school work, so they all just kind of hunkered down while she and my dad went from window to window, trying to see what was out there.

My dad said Miss Thomas was the best teacher he ever had and very pragmatic. She knew the kids were overly excited, and if the bear came up to the schoolhouse, she might have some hysterical kids on her hands, so she told them if they promised to not be afraid, she would read them a story. This was a real treat, something they all loved and that she saved for special occasions, like when they all got their work done early or were especially good.

They were in the middle of reading Huckleberry Finn, so she started back in. In the meantime, while reading, she motioned my dad up to her desk. She whispered for him to go around and make sure all the windows were locked and to close the curtains so nothing could see in, then to go lock the door in the outer room.

My dad did all this, but when he got to the back room, he decided to take a quick look outside and see if he could make anything out. He saw that the horses had broken the top rails of the corral and were long gone. He knew they would go home, and if the parents saw them, they would come looking for the kids, and that would be a good thing.

As he was stepping back in, he caught a glimpse, just for a second, of something dark going around the back of the school. He stood there watching, hoping to see what it was. He told me it happened so fast he couldn't believe it, but all of a sudden the thing had come around the other side and was behind him. My dad was partway in the school and partway out, and this thing was almost on him before he managed to jump in and slam the door and lock it. It was long enough for him to get a good look at it.

My dad would never really describe what he saw, except to say he wished he'd never seen it, because it gave him nightmares for years. He even talked about it when he was dying and regretted ever knowing the thing existed. It had a very profound impact on him. All he would say was that it was a human gorilla and very cunning.

He went running back into the main room, but even though he was basically in shock, he didn't want to scare the kids, so he asked the teacher to come back with him. He wanted her to help him barricade the door, and he told her why. He said she was stunned but seemed to believe him, especially after the little girl has said she'd seen a gorilla.

The creature never did bother them, but they were too terrified to go outside, so after they blocked the door, Miss Thomas just kept reading Huckleberry Finn. My dad had told her the horses were gone, and she knew sooner or later worried parents would show up.

Sure enough, the first one to show was the mom of one of the ranch kids. She drove up to the school and promptly turned around and drove back into town, where she went into the little store there and told the owner there was a giant monkey at the schoolhouse. He got his shotgun and drove back with her, but didn't see anything.

By then, another mom had shown up and knocked on the schoolhouse door, where Miss Thomas happily let her in. Between her and the other mom and store owner, they managed to evacuate the school and take the kids back to the store. The store owner then went back to the school to tell the other parents what was going on when they showed up.

Well, my grandma was next to show, and the store owner told her what had happened just as the creature let out a scream that shook the ground. You can bet they didn't stick around.

Eventually, everything got sorted out and all the kids made it home. The consensus was to shut the school down until they could figure out what was going on. Since it was late spring already, it wasn't that big of a deal, as this was back before school districts had rules out the wazoo about how many days a kid had to be in school and all that.

So, that was the end of this thing terrorizing the school-house, but it wasn't the end of its career in the area. It hung around for a month, going from ranch to ranch and scaring people. It never came back to our ranch, although the Kid said she saw it from the rear while it was climbing a nearby hill.

But it did scare a lot of people. It would peek in windows and whack on the sides of houses. It would stampede livestock and go into barns and eat the horses' grain. It just ended up causing a lot of havoc and chaos. All the kids in the valley were kept indoors.

Finally, everyone had had enough and a hunting party was put together. Everyone was terrified of it, and the horses wouldn't go near it, so my dad thought it was more to make everyone think something was being done, when in reality, nobody knew what to do.

So, about eight ranchers took off one morning on horse-back, looking for what they were now calling Old Brown, a name they made up to not scare the kids when they talked about it. They rode up and down the valley hunting through the willows, with no luck. Finally, along at about sundown, someone saw it running up the side of a distant hill, and they all let go with their firepower, though it was actually too far away to hit.

My dad figured that scared it away, because it never was seen again. He told me that, in Old Brown's defense, the creature never harmed anyone or anything, not even the calves that would have been so easy to kill. He figured it was old and hungry.

Who knows, maybe it was the last of its kind in the area and lonely. But to his dying day, my dad said he wished he'd never seen the thing.

[17] The Jaws of Life

This story was told by a gal named Kathy over a nice trout dinner along the Yellowstone River up in Paradise Valley, Montana. There's no place like the Yellowstone for enjoying fresh grilled trout along the sparkling water while listening to a good Bigfoot story. —Rusty

We've all heard the statistics on how lots of people have car accidents, but I believe we're usually in denial that it could happen to us. At least I was until the odds caught up with me, and I also believe that the odds of being rescued in the fashion I was are astronomical.

I still have no idea why it all happened, but maybe there really isn't a reason, it's just how life is sometimes, how things come together.

I'm an audiologist with a Utah state agency, and I was on my way to the little southeastern Utah town of Blanding to test some of the kids there. The state tries to get all the kids tested, and Blanding is close to the White Mountain Ute Reservation, so I would go down there periodically to test those little kids.

I was based in Salt Lake City, so it's a bit of a drive down there, over 300 miles, and I always have to spend a night or two away from home in a motel. I think the fact that I decided to drive down there after work instead of waiting until the next day was why I ran off the road, as I was tired.

Well, once you get around 20 miles out of Monticello, a pretty little mountain town not far north of Blanding, you come to a pretty good grade. I don't know what it's called, but I'm sure it has a name. It's like a small mountain pass, and has a few good drop offs. I was lucky that I ran off the inside of the road instead of the outside. It's rugged country with no houses or signs of human habitation for a long ways, in fact, there's basically nothing for the entire 45 miles between Moab and Monticello.

It was late when I got to this pass, which crosses the flanks of the Abajo Mountains, and it had been dark for a couple of hours, even though it was summer and the days were long. I've gone over that pass lots of times in the winter, and it can be really icy, and you have to watch out for deer.

Well, the deer are usually up in the higher country in the summer, but sure enough, I came around a corner, and standing right there in the middle of the road were two deer. My headlights blinded them and they just stood there.

I was going about 65, fast enough I knew it would really damage my car if I hit them, not to mention the poor deer. I really sat on the brakes, burning rubber, but they just stood there, so my last recourse was to swerve. By then, I'd probably slowed down to about 50, but it was still fast enough that I lost control. Basically, I overcorrected.

I remember when I was young and my dad was teaching me how to drive, he told me that overcorrecting was the cause of many accidents, so I was aware you should never do this. But I was really tired, and my judgement was off.

I'll never forget the feeling of flying off the highway and literally catching air as I went over an embankment, crashing through the aspens and landing below.

My final thoughts were OK, now I know how I'm going to die. I wasn't particularly afraid. I just knew it was the end, and I wondered if they would ever find my body down there in the trees, down below the highway.

That's all I remember, and I don't know how long I was unconscious, but I must have hit my head on the steering wheel, because I was definitely knocked out.

I woke up with something warm and sticky running down my face, and I could smell blood. I sat there for awhile, not even sure who I was or where, then I gradually began to recall what had happened. I was surprised I was still alive.

I reached up and could feel there was a big cut on my forehead, which was the source of the blood. I then kind of did a body check to see if I had any injuries, and I could feel my shoulders and neck aching, so I figured I'd had a bit of whiplash, but everything else seemed OK. I was glad I'd been wearing my seatbelt. But I felt all twisted around for some reason.

I reached over and managed to unhook my seatbelt, then I got my jacket from the back seat and held it to my head, finally stopping the bleeding. Even though the cut hurt like heck, I could tell it was just a surface wound. Since surface wounds bleed a lot, it took awhile before I could get it stopped, and my jacket was soaked with blood.

But I got it stopped, and I was beginning to think I was going to be OK and survive. My next thoughts were that I needed to get out of the car and back up to the highway where someone would see me and help me. I was woozy and groggy from hitting my head, but I knew I had to get out.

OK, now came the hard part. The car had landed on its side, and that just happened to be the driver's side, so there was no way I could open that door to get out. That's why I felt all twisted around, I was basically on my side.

I was going to have to crawl up to the passenger door and force it open, while gravity held it down. But I was driving a little two-door Honda, so I didn't think it would be too difficult, as the door wasn't like some big heavy pickup door or anything.

But climbing up the car wasn't easy. I kept sliding back down into the driver's seat, and I couldn't get any leverage to open the door. Every time I would slide back, I would ache and hurt even more, and I was still fighting wanting to go to sleep from the concussion I'd got when I hit the steering wheel.

After about a half-dozen tries, I finally managed to wedge myself into the seat enough to be able to reach up and unlock the door then push on it. But nothing happened. It wouldn't budge.

OK, I next managed to turn myself around and use my feet to push, using a lot of force. But that didn't work either.

I don't know how many times and angles and ways I tried to open that door, but it was no use, it was stuck. There was nothing I could do to open it.

I just crumpled back down into the driver's side and started crying. It was all too much. I couldn't believe I was stuck in my own car, down in a ravine off the highway where no one could see me.

I must've drifted off, because when I woke again, it was daylight. I was now really stiff and sore from the bruising I'd got, the cut on my head throbbed, and I was getting a bad headache. I needed to get out of that car.

I was now feeling desperate. I knew my only recourse at this point was to break out the window. The car seemed to be dead, and when I turned the key the automatic window opener wouldn't work.

I started looking around for some tool to use, but there was nothing. Oh, man, I was starting to get claustrophobic and panicky. On top of that, I was hungry and thirsty. I knew they would be missing me at the clinic, but they would have no idea where to look. And I couldn't find anything to break the window with.

I just sat there, it all sinking in. Instead of dying in a car crash, I was going to die of thirst, and I had about three or four days to sit there and slowly let that sink in. I'm a realist, and I had no illusions about what was ahead of me. It was going to be a really bad way to go.

Well, I guess that thought motivated me, because I found myself desperately trying to break the automatic shift lever off the steering wheel assembly, and I eventually was able to kick it off with my feet. How I twisted around to do that is beyond me, as I felt like I was sitting in a hole, and even trying to move was getting difficult from being so stiff.

OK, now I had a tool, a big plastic stick-like thing, the shifter. I managed to climb back up enough to start whacking on the window with it, but of course, safety glass isn't easy to break, and the stick had no effect at all.

I tried over and over to break that window, then I tried the front glass with the same effect. It seemed even thicker, so I gave up on that and went back to trying to break the side window. After numerous attempts, I crumpled back into a heap and cried.

I needed something metal, but there wasn't anything at all in the car. I was stuck. It was hopeless. I needed to rest again after all the effort, and I could feel myself getting weaker.

Now I just sat there, drifting in and out of unconsciousness, thinking of my life and all the stupid mistakes I'd made and wondering why I had to die like this. I was only 43 years old, and I had a husband and two kids at home. I wondered if they would do OK without me.

I just sat there all day, thinking like that between bouts of trying to break out that window and yelling for help, even though I knew no one could hear me through the closed windows.

I tried everything, even kicking the glass, but nothing worked. I just couldn't get enough leverage, as it was too far above me. I was desperate, but there was nothing I could do. And to make things worse, it was getting hot and stuffy in the car.

I hoped someone would maybe see my skid marks and come looking for me, but nobody came. It was the longest day of my life, and it changed me completely. I now value each day and try to live it fully. But at that time, I didn't really think I was going to have very many more days to live, yet alone to live fully. It seemed like a bad cosmic joke, with me at the brunt of it, and I didn't find it very funny.

I must've slept again, because when I woke up, it was dark. I was now terribly thirsty, as I hadn't had anything to drink since the evening before, and the heat in the car was bad. My throat was soon so dry I almost couldn't swallow, and my lips were starting to crack.

I was very light-headed at this point, and what happened next I would say wasn't real, except it had to be, as there's no other reason I'm here and alive now. But at the time, I thought, well, this is what happens when you die of dehydration. Your mind plays weird tricks on you, makes you think you're going to be rescued, but you're not. It's all from your brain shutting down, so don't get your hopes up.

I have no idea what time of night it was, but it had to be late. I could see the stars directly above me through the passenger window. I sat there, kind of twisted sideways, looking at the stars and thinking I was so insignificant, my life was so worthless, when suddenly the stars disappeared. Another weird trick of the mind, I thought, but then they reappeared just as suddenly. It then dawned on me that something was out there and had been looking in at me.

Normally, this would have scared me to death, but since
I figured I was already a goner, I just felt a simple curiosity.
What had looked in and blocked my view of the stars?

Now it was back, and I could make out the outline of
a very large head barely backlit by the millions of stars in
the clear night sky. I sat there, looking at it as it studied me,
and I could tell it was covered with hair from the way it
looked all fuzzy. It appeared to have no ears, and it was big.
That head filled up the entire window!

OK, what happened next would normally terrify me,
but I just remember wondering how that worked—this
thing suddenly had glowing red eyes! Where it hadn't
before, now its eyes were kind of radiating out this bright
red light, and it seemed to light up the car. It was like it had
two glowing cigarette lighters in its head.

I knew it was studying me and trying to figure me out,
but I wasn't at all afraid. In fact, it kind of relaxed me,
knowing there was another living creature around.

At no time during any of this did I feel any fear at all.
In fact, I remember smiling at it and wondering if it would
think I was showing my teeth in aggression. But then I
laughed at myself. How could anything be afraid of me in
the helpless position I was in?

Well, now there was another big head looking in. So,
there were two of them, I thought, wondering what they
made of this whole deal, a puny helpless human in a
wrecked car, unable to hardly even move.

OK, I take back what I said about having no fear. This
part really scared me. Suddenly, the car began to rock, with
me rocking inside with it, back and forth. I was totally terrified! But soon, the car was righted. These creatures had sat

my car back on its wheels, and how they did that I have no idea, yet alone why. Were they trying to help me?

This took awhile to set in, for me to realize what had happened. I was no longer scrunched down against the driver's door, but sat up like one normally would in a car. It was a huge relief to have the pressure gone. I was now again unafraid, knowing what they'd done. In fact, I was somewhat elated!

But the elation didn't last long when I remembered I couldn't get out. I tried to open the driver's door, but it was totally crumpled inward from the crash and wouldn't budge. I tried the passenger door again, but no luck. In my frustration, I started kicking it as hard as I could, yelling and cussing. This ended in another bout of hopeless tears, as I was so weak I had trouble kicking.

But suddenly, I could hear the sound of metal tearing. The car door was being wrenched off! These creatures pulled that door off that car like you or I would pop the flip top of a can. Fresh air flowed into the car and was so sweet I could taste it. I could breathe again! And now I was free!

I scooted over and looked out of the car and didn't see anything, but I had goosebumps on my arms. Whatever they were, they were gone.

It was still dark, and now I began to wonder if I should try to climb the hill or wait until daylight. I decided to wait, as I didn't need any more accidents. But now I could stretch out in the car and sleep.

I got comfortable and went to sleep, with no thought of harm coming to me from the creatures. I knew they were helping me. They were like living Jaws of Life, those special tools used to rescue people from cars, and I knew they had to be very strong to do what they'd just done.

The next morning I woke early, extremely thirsty and hungry, and managed to drag myself up the slope, where a man in a passing car stopped and helped me. After a few days in the hospital in Monticello, I was soon on my way home with my husband.

I later received a call from the patrolman who investigated the accident, and he asked a lot of questions. He was especially interested in how the car door was wrenched off and thrown twenty feet. I just told him someone came by and helped me, but I don't remember much about it. I didn't get a ticket.

Not long after, I had a journalist call me. When she asked how the car door had been wrenched off, I just told her I was in shock and didn't remember, but someone had helped me out.

My accident made the front page of the Salt Lake Newspaper. The headline read, "Woman Mysteriously Rescued from Wrecked Car by Strangers."

They may be strangers, but I hope they stay mysterious forever. There are some creatures out there who are better off hidden, but I'll forever be grateful to that pair who cared enough to save my life and give me a second chance.

EIGHTEEN PACK OF BIGFOOT CAMPFIRE STORIES

[18] The Fire Lookout

This story came my way one stormy night high in the lake country of Grand Mesa, Colorado. If I recall, there were six of us sitting around the fire, trying to stay warm as a storm blew through.

A fellow named Gary told the story, and we got so caught up in it we nearly started a forest fire, which would've been ironic as heck, considering the setting of his story. The winds were coming through as he told it, and we neglected to kill our campfire until sparks were flying around, as he had us so intrigued. When the story was finished, we all hastily jumped up and put the fire out. —Rusty

When one thinks of fire towers, they probably think of places like Washington, Idaho, and Oregon where there are vast forests, but I worked one short season as a fire tower lookout in, of all places, the state of Utah. I was fresh out of college, and it was 1979.

Even though I had a degree in forestry, I managed to get the job mostly because my uncle knew the right people.

One of his buddies was the chief ranger for the Ashley National Forest, which is where the tower is located.

I ended up in the Ute Mountain Lookout, the first lookout tower ever built in Utah. There, I lived fifty feet above the ground in a small 14-by-14 foot structure on white wooden braces that was built by the Civilian Conservation Corps in 1937.

It's still there and is now on the National Register of Historic Places. If you know the area, it's not far from Flaming Gorge in the northeastern part of the state. You can drive up the mountain right to it.

I loved it there. I had never been in such a remote place for so long, and the solitude was really great. You have to be the right kind of personality to like being a lookout, mostly a loner type, at least enough of a loner to enjoy the summers out in the middle of nowhere.

I would stand on the deck outside and scan the area for smoke. I had a 360 degree view from where I was, at an altitude of almost 9,000 feet. I could see over 200 miles in any direction, well into Wyoming and Colorado, as well as the majority of the Uinta Mountains.

When I spotted smoke, I would use an Osborne Fire Finder, a type of alidade, to get a directional bearing, then I would radio fire crews. But most of the time I didn't see anything except wildlife and lots of weather. You've never experienced lightning until you've been high on a mountain top in a fire tower.

The Uinta Mountains are a really unique range, in that it's the only mountain range in the lower U.S. that runs east-west. The Uintas are really rugged and have lots of lakes. A lot of it is wilderness, so you can get there only by foot. It was once the land of the Utes and Shoshones.

So there I was, a fire lookout, high in the wild Uintas, though not real far from the little town of Manila. I had lots of visitors that summer, some just coming to see the tower and some needing directions or help of various kinds (usually nothing very serious). Such is the life of a fire lookout.

But towards the end of the summer, I had visitors I've never seen the likes of since, visitors that put an end to my wanting much to do with the forests, although I did continue in forestry, but more from an office perspective.

My typical day would be about as mellow as can be, and I often had to pinch myself, as I just couldn't believe I was getting paid to be out in this beautiful place. I would get up and make some coffee on my little propane stove, then go sit on the deck way up in the air and scan for smoke with my binoculars.

After I was satisfied there weren't any new fires started during the night, I would go back inside and make bacon and eggs, then go back out and eat, watching clouds and whatever else captured my interest. Deer and elk would wander nearby, and sometimes I would be lucky enough to see a moose or two. And if I was really lucky, a black bear would amble by.

The neat thing about it was that these animals didn't know I was watching them and were totally like they would be without fear of humans. I saw some pretty interesting behavior, like does stomping their feet at each other over a nice patch of grass. I once even saw a momma beaver grooming her young one, using her claws and teeth. That was something else. How they ended up on the top of Ute Mountain was beyond me, but there are a lot of nearby lakes. It was a rare day that I didn't see some kind of animal come through.

One of those lakes is called Spirit Lake and is just a few miles away. In fact, the road to the lookout tower is off the Spirit Lake Road. I don't know why it's called Spirit Lake, but local legend has it that Wakara, a famous Ute leader, fell in love with a Ute girl named Sasquina and married her, but she came up missing.

She was supposedly turned into a big white elk that came walking out of Spirit Lake, wearing a necklace that Wakara had made for her. But after what happened, I wondered if Spirit Lake hadn't really been named for another kind of spirit, one more easily seen as a devil than an Indian princess.

But on with the story, I just wanted to give you some background so you'd have a feel for this unique place. My days were filled with looking for smoke and watching the weather and wildlife.

Well, one day, on towards autumn and the end of my tenure there, I noticed movement in the forest around the tower. The tower sat in the middle of a clearing, and I don't know if it was naturally that way or had been cleared to reduce the fire hazard, so what I was seeing was kind of a ways over from me. I knew there was some kind of animal over there in the trees, but I wasn't sure exactly what.

Before long, a small herd of about twenty deer came on across the clearing from one side of the mountain and disappeared down the other. They weren't acting normal at all, but more like deer do during hunting season, when they're trying to get away from somebody. They were acting a bit panicked, but not enough to run.

They were soon gone, and that was the last wildlife I saw for a week or so.

Every night, I would go out on the deck and star gaze. The night sky is incredible up there, as there was no light pollution. The closest city was Salt Lake, and it was far away, 100 miles, clear over on the other side of the Wasatch Range.

That same day that the deer came through, I was out watching the night sky, hoping to see the occasional satellite, and I noticed that something was different. It took awhile to put my finger on it, but it finally dawned on me that it was deathly still.

The only other time I've ever experienced this kind of stillness was once when I was in Oklahoma right before a big tornado came through. The barometric pressure had dropped and all nature was aware of something big about to happen. Well, this night was the same way, and I wondered if a big front was coming in or something, though my battery-powered weather radio had called for good weather.

I sat there for the longest time, feeling the difference, and it left me a bit out of balance. It felt like something was wrong there in my personal paradise, but I had no idea what it could be.

The next two days were calm and quiet, but the deathly stillness continued. I was half afraid to climb down the tower and go to my old pickup, which sat below and had water jugs in the back. I felt like nesting up there, where I was safe. I'd never felt before like I should stay in the tower.

I finally made myself climb down the long staircase and get a five-gallon jug, as I was running low. I spent the rest of the day scoping for smoke and doing crossword puzzles, feeling out of sorts and out of balance.

That night, something woke me up. I didn't know what, as I heard no noises or anything. I wondered if it were my intuition telling me a fire was starting somewhere. There had been no clouds or lightning, so if there were, it had to be man-made.

I got up and opened the door out to the deck and scanned the terrain in the dark, looking for flames. I saw nothing, but then I heard it, a coughing sound coming from the forest not too far from the edge of the clearing.

Bears can make coughing sounds, so I figured I had a bear visitor. The knowledge that they can climb and could easily come up to my stronghold didn't set well, but it was nothing new. I was armed and knew it was highly unlikely one would visit. I was very careful with my cooking, so there was no need for them to associate the tower with food.

I finally turned and went back inside and back to bed, but I had trouble sleeping. My intuition was telling me something was going on, but I didn't know it then, I just felt out of sorts.

The next morning, all was well, no signs of bears. I climbed down to my pickup again and looked around for tracks, but found nothing.

But that morning, while I was scanning for fires while drinking my morning coffee, something very unusual caught my eye. There, in the pines about a hundred feet or so from the edge of the clearing, was something up in the trees. I couldn't quite make it out, but it looked like some-one had built a platform up high, and these weren't small trees, but old-growth and maybe forty feet tall.

I looked hard with my high-powered binoculars, and I could make out two of these platform things. They were pretty good sized, mostly round, maybe eight feet in di-ameter, and looked like something had dragged broken limbs into a natural cleft in the branches up high and put in a framework of big branches that still had the needles attached, then laced smaller branches into the larger ones. They looked like giant bird nests, side by side, as weird as that sounds. It was hard to tell, but they looked like they were filled with soft twigs and leaves.

For the life of me, I couldn't figure this out. Bear hunters would sometimes build permanent tree stands, but not this big and not way up high in the trees.

I decided to go have a look. Maybe they were old Ute burial platforms, as I'd heard the Utes of long ago built platforms in trees and left their dead there. It could be an important archaeological find.

As I was climbing down the stairs, however, it occurred to me that Ute platforms would probably be really old and unlikely to stand the ravages of time. The winds would tear them down, and the elements would destroy them. It was highly unlikely that any would still survive, and these looked freshly made. In fact, I knew I would have noticed them long before now if they'd been there all summer. And whatever they were, I really couldn't check them out with-out climbing high into the trees.

I turned and climbed back up the tower. The nests kind of gave me the creeps, to be honest, and I was once again afraid to leave the safety of my perch up high.

I woke up in a cold sweat that night, around midnight. I was dreaming that someone was calling my name, trying to lure me into a giant nest in a tree, someone bad. As I lay there, my heart pounding, I heard a sound from outside. I typically left a couple of windows open to catch the cool night breezes.

There was someone standing beneath the tower, calling out. I thought I was still dreaming, but deep inside I knew I wasn't. Maybe it was a lost hiker or someone who had driven up and needed help. I quietly got up and pulled on my clothes. For some reason, I knew not to turn on the light.

I very stealthily crept out onto the deck, trying to stay hidden around the edge of the building, my back pressed tight against it. There it was again, someone calling out! I felt a chill go all the way down my neck clear into my boots.

There was something down there, and it sounded like they were trying to yell out, "Hey!" but what came out instead was something like, "Huhey," like they were imitating a human but didn't quite have it down. The voice was way more husky sounding than any human I'd ever heard, and it carried.

Now I could hear sticks crunching below me. I was fifty feet up in the air, but the stairs up here were wide and very accessible, a pretty easy climb. I felt very vulnerable, and I needed to know more, to know what was going on.

I poked my head around the corner of the building and

tried to see down through a space in the decking. I could see something dark, like a huge shadow. At first I thought it was a tree, then I remembered there weren't any trees next to the building, and then it moved.

There was something down there, and it was on two legs, moving around and calling out, as if trying to get me to come out. My instincts were on full alert, and I'd seen all I needed to see. I slipped back into the building, locked the door, and kind of hunkered down, wishing I had curtains on the windows.

I then remembered two windows were open, so I quietly walked over and latched them. I then gathered my rifle, made sure it was loaded, and sat in the shadows in the corner, where I was least likely to be seen.

Now whatever it was, it was shaking the building! This was a big structure, yet I could feel the wood groan a bit and move ever so slightly. It had to be really strong to do that! The only time I'd ever felt the building move at all was in high winds. I'd been up there in a couple of big storms when the anemometer recorded 70 m.p.h. winds. That had buffeted the building around, just like this creature was doing. My heart sank as I realized the strength I was witnessing.

I decided I was in extreme danger. I crawled over to the hand-held radio and called out, whispering, but nobody seemed to be up to hear me.

I sat there all night, kind of dozing off, but nothing else happened. The next morning, I woke, all stiff and sore. I was still afraid, even in broad daylight. It was a feeling I never want to feel again.

I tried to pretend everything was normal, and I got up and made coffee. I stepped out onto the deck and started glassing the horizon, looking for smoke. That's when I noticed movement in the trees—there were two dark things in the nests!

No way! I thought I was dreaming, but I could definitely see two creatures in the nests high in the trees. I tried to make out what they were, but all I could tell was that they were big and had dark fur.

I had to get out of there! I radioed headquarters, and now someone answered. I wasn't even sure what to say, but I managed to get out that I was coming out and the tower would be unmanned. When asked why, I just said I was sick.

I then gathered a few things and headed down the stairs full throttle, as nothing was going to stop me from leaving. I was down off that tower in record time, and unlocked my truck and threw my things in. All I had grabbed were a few things I could easily carry and that couldn't be replaced, like my wallet, my journal, my binoculars, and my warm jacket.

As I got into the truck, I noticed there were footprints all over the place, big footprints. Whatever it was had walked all around the tower several times, as if thinking about coming up, then deciding not to. I started the truck and peeled out, happy to be on my way down the mountain. It was then that I noticed my side mirrors had been torn off, just pulled off like they were pop-tops on a beer can.

I didn't stop until I got to Vernal, then I went into the forest building. My friend Eric, a full-time ranger, was working that day, and he seemed surprised to see me, even though I told everyone I was coming down.

H asked how I was feeling and if I needed a place to stay until I got better. I think he figured I had a bad cold or something, and he and his wife had a nice little place there in town.

I took him up on his offer, as I wanted some time to think things over. I wanted to decide if I had it in me to go back and finish the season, or if I should just go on home. After all, nothing had really happened, not really.

I'd been to his place before, so I just went on out and made myself at home, as his wife was also at work. Before long, I was fast asleep on their couch.

Well, when Eric came home after work, he and his wife made me a nice spaghetti dinner, and afterwards, over a beer, I decided to come clean and tell them what had really happened.

After hearing my story, Eric looked visibly upset, and his wife was white as a sheet. I was now starting to feel a bit guilty, like I had run off from my job, and here I was scaring these nice people, when it was probably just a bear. But what Eric told me confirmed I'd done the right thing.

He said the high Uintas had been the site of numerous Bigfoot sightings, and he theorized that Spirit Lake was on a migration route, as every year in the early fall, the creatures were sighted near the lake. After a few weeks, the sightings would end until the next fall, but there were a number of locals who now refused to go into the Uintas at any time of the year.

Two years previous, the fire lookout had actually been visited by a Bigfoot that climbed straight up the tower and broke in, taking food while the lookout watched, cowering and petrified. It hadn't harmed him, but the guy left immediately and never came back.

I was relieved to hear I hadn't been dreaming. I felt bad for Eric, as he had to work in the forest, but he seemed OK with it, though his wife didn't. He had put in for a transfer for her sake, but he kind of hoped to see a Bigfoot before he left. He was fascinated by them, and it was hard for me to convey the terror they had inspired in me. He was going to go back up to Ute Tower and look at the nests.

After a restful night at Eric's, I went into the main forestry office and resigned, telling my uncle's friend, the chief ranger, exactly why. He offered to take me out to get the rest of my stuff, but I had no intention of ever going back. He seemed understanding, as if he'd been through it before, and to my knowledge, he never mentioned it to my uncle.

Eric did go up to see the nests, and he got the rest of my stuff for me and shut the tower down for the season. He said it gave him the creeps, and his wife wasn't too happy he'd gone up there.

Years later, I was reading about primates and found an article on how they build nests in trees, just like the Bigfoot appeared to have done. The nests are safer than being on the ground and are also free of insects and parasites that one finds crawling around in the dirt in tropical climates. Nests are also warmer, and anthropologists believe that humans once lived in tree nests, primarily for safety. They think that humans came down from the trees when we learned how to make fires for safety.

So, I guess if I ever do go back to the Uintas, maybe I'll stay in a nest, though my lookout tower did kind of feel that way. I sure enjoyed the views, at least until the neighborhood went to the birds.

About the Author

• •

Rusty Wilson grew up in the state of Washington, in the heart of Bigfoot country. He didn't know a thing about Bigfoot until he got lost at the age of six and was then found and subsequently adopted by a kindly Bigfoot family.

He lived with them until he was 16, when they finally gave up on ever socializing him into Bigfoot ways (he hated garlic and pancakes, refused to sleep in a nest, wouldn't hunt wild pigs, and on top of it all, his feet were small).

His Bigfoot family then sent him off to Evergreen State College in nearby Olympia, thinking it would be liberal enough to take care of a kid with few redeeming qualities, plus they liked the thick foliage around the college and figured Rusty could live there, saving them money for housing.

At Evergreen, Rusty studied wildlife biology, eventually returning to the wilds, after first learning to read and write and regale everyone with his wild tales. He eventually became a flyfishing guide, and during his many travels in the wilds, he collected stories from others who have had contact with Bigfoot, also known as Sasquatch.

Because of his background, Rusty is considered to be the world's foremost Bigfoot expert (at least so by himself, if not by anyone else). He's spent many a fun evening around campfires with his clients, telling stories. Some of those clients had some pretty good stories of their own.

If you've enjoyed this, you might want to read *Rusty Wilson's Bigfoot Campfire Stories*, as well as *Rusty Wilson's More Bigfoot Campfire Stories*, and *Rusty Wilson's Favorite Bigfoot Campfire Stories, all* available in print at amazon.com or your favorite bookstore. Rusty also has various ebooks available at yellowcatbooks.com, amazon.com, bn.com, and various other ebook retailers.

You can follow and communicate with Rusty at his blog at rustybigfoot.blogspot.com. And check out the Bigfoot Headquarters at yellowcatbooks.com.

And if you enjoyed this book, you will also like *The Ghost Rock Cafe*, a Bigfoot mystery by Chinle Miller. Also available at yellowcatbooks.com, bn.com, and Amazon.com.

Whether you're a Bigfoot believer or not, we hope you enjoyed these tall tales...or are they really true stories?

Only Rusty and his fellow storytellers know for sure.

Made in the USA
Columbia, SC
22 September 2021